THE MOFFAT MUSEUM

OTHER YEARLING BOOKS YOU WILL ENJOY:

THE MOFFATS, *Eleanor Estes*
RUFUS M., *Eleanor Estes*
THE MIDDLE MOFFAT, *Eleanor Estes*
HAPPY LITTLE FAMILY, *Rebecca Caudill*
SCHOOLHOUSE IN THE WOODS, *Rebecca Caudill*
SCHOOLROOM IN THE PARLOR, *Rebecca Caudill*
UP AND DOWN THE RIVER, *Rebecca Caudill*
SATURDAY COUSINS, *Rebecca Caudill*
A CERTAIN SMALL SHEPHERD, *Rebecca Caudill*
BETSY'S BUSY SUMMER, *Carolyn Haywood*

YEARLING BOOKS/YOUNG YEARLINGS/YEARLING CLASSICS are designed especially to entertain and enlighten young people. Patricia Reilly Giff, consultant to this series, received the bachelor's degree from Marymount College. She holds the master's degree in history from St. John's University, and a Professional Diploma in Reading from Hofstra University. She was a teacher and reading consultant for many years, and is the author of numerous books for young readers.

For a complete listing of all Yearling titles,
write to Dell Readers Service,
P.O. Box 1045, South Holland, IL 60473.

THE
MOFFAT
MUSEUM

BY

ELEANOR ESTES

ILLUSTRATED BY THE AUTHOR

A Yearling Book

Published by
Dell Publishing
a division of
Bantam Doubleday Dell Publishing Group, Inc.
666 Fifth Avenue
New York, New York 10103

ISBN: 0-440-70029-9

Reprinted by arrangement with Harcourt Brace Jovanovich, Publishers

Printed in the United States of America

August 1989

10 9 8 7 6 5 4 3 2 1

KRI

To Carolyn, Gillis, and Ted

CONTENTS

1

A SPECIAL MUSEUM

THE MOFFATS SHOULD HAVE A MUSEUM! SUDDENLY THIS
idea popped into Jane's head as she was sitting alone on the
back stoop of the little gray house at 12 Ashbellows Place in
Cranbury, where the Moffats lived.

It was a very hot day in June. Jane cupped her chin in her
hands. She hadn't been thinking of anything in particular, just
dreaming, just listening to the buzzing of the bees in the honeysuckle that spread along the fence of the house next door. This
part of the fence was very close to a barn in the Moffats' back-

3

yard, and some honeysuckle had climbed up onto the roof of the barn.

Absentmindedly, Jane scrutinized the barn . . . weather-beaten, wide open at the front. The doors had been taken off years ago and were propped against the barn on the honeysuckle side. Therefore, you could always see inside, though there wasn't much to see. The main thing was an ancient sleigh, an old-fashioned sleigh, not very large. It was already in the barn when the Moffats moved here from the Yellow House on New Dollar Street.

Jane began to think about the sleigh. Really, a sleigh like this should be in a museum.

It was then that the idea of the Moffats having a museum popped into her head. A museum in the barn! A special museum, a collection of things that had been important to one, some, or all of the Moffats. THE MOFFAT MUSEUM!

In this town named Cranbury, where three thousand people lived . . . it said so on a sign at the Cumberland Avenue Bridge: "Entering Cranbury, population, 3,000" . . . there was not one museum! There were schools, stores, houses, the library, the Town Hall, a green with two churches on it; and there were little brooks, large fields, some cows, and plenty of places to go to, take walks to or take a trolley car to: Savin

Rock, Lighthouse Point, and more. But no museum of any sort
. . . art, science, or anything! "There are museums," Joey had
told her, "for every known thing somewhere in the world."

"Museums," mused Jane, "for every known thing!" She remembered a teacher she once had who said there was a museum in a town in England just for shoes, shoes from the earli-
est time to the present.

Joey liked best a museum in Washington: "first" things . . .
first airplane, first steam locomotive, first trolley, everything
"first!"

"Ah!" murmured Jane, standing up now and going close to
the barn. She addressed it. "Barn! You may soon become the
first and only museum in Cranbury. No museum here? We'll
change that! 'First' things or any treasured things of any Moffat!"

Wait till the boys came home and heard this! Wow! Where
were they anyway? Here was a museum all in her head. She
needed Joey and Rufus or someone to tell her plan to. Oh, if
only Nancy Stokes, her best friend, had not gone off to Maine
so early! Nancy's house was on the next street, but her apple
orchard garden and backyard and Jane's backyard were sep-
arated only by a green wooden fence. Nancy's mother had let
the girls take one wide green board out, put hinges on it, and
it had become a secret door between the two yards.

Oh, how Jane missed Nancy! Missed seeing her squeeze through the secret door, missed hearing her whistle . . . "Peewee!" like the sound of the peewee bird.

No sense wishing for Nancy. She just wasn't here. Anyway, the boys were more important right now. She needed other Moffats.

She looked past the house and to the street. No sign of them.

This place in front of the barn and near their neighbor's fence was a perfect place to view whoever might come to visit the museum. Jane smiled happily. People might come from far away, from Montowese, or even from England, to see how a museum in Cranbury, Connecticut, compared with a shoe museum somewhere in their land!

Jane stretched out her arms as though welcoming a large part of the population to The Moffat Museum . . . if news of it got around, that is.

"Oh, pooh!" she said. "This museum is really for us Moffats, to have in it loved things, really just for us and a friend or two, and their friends' friends."

Again Jane held her arms out to extend a welcome to a friend or a friend of a friend.

In the distance she could hear the tinkling sound of a ragman and his voice, as from far, far away, yet coming nearer: "Cash paid for rags . . . cash paid for rags . . ." She thought nothing of it, no more than of the humming of the bees she had been listening to.

What was nice was that while she was stretching out her arms, welcoming an unknown into The Moffat Museum, her two brothers did come riding lickety-split up the narrow walk. Rufus rang the bell and rang the bell, urging Joey to go faster and faster!

You'd have thought he was going to ride right through her and into the barn, out the other end, and then through the secret gate. But he put on his brakes in the nick of time, making the dirt fly.

"Don't do that," said Jane. "It scares me. Feel my heart, how it's pounding. I have gooseflesh, see?"

"Oinck! Oinck!" said Rufus. "But what were you doing there, standing like a statue, holding out your arms?"

"Statue!" exclaimed Jane. "You're getting close. What do you see there? Look!" She pointed to the barn.

"The barn!" said the boys. "So what!"

"Oh, no!" said Jane. "What you see there is . . . or will be soon, when we get going . . . a *museum*! The Moffat Museum!"

The boys liked the idea right away. Both of them did.

"Yes!" said Jane eagerly. "A museum! The one and only museum in the town of Cranbury."

"Population circa MMM," Rufus put in.

"It's going to be a museum just for Moffat things!" said Jane.

"Bikey!" said Rufus. He ran to the side of the yard behind the raspberry bushes, where he had a garage for his special things. But Bikey, as they all fondly called this bicycle, was gone!

Silence! Then into the silence came the sound of the ragman's tinkling little tin bells. Suddenly the bells stopped. A horse neighed and stomped his feet. The ragman stopped his chanting, "Cash paid for rags!" He bought more things than old rags, though. Junk, just junk, like an old baby carriage, or an old bicycle?

Some people might call Bikey junk. That's what the children thought.

They rushed to the street. They were right! There was Mama about to hand Bikey over to the ragman as a piece of "junk."

"Ten cents," they heard the man say.

"All right," they heard Mama say.

"Oh, no!" shouted the three children. "Mama! Don't sell our bike! It's valuable. Every one of us has learned to ride on it! It's like a pet!"

"Here!" said Rufus, stripping off his sailor blouse. "Take this instead!"

Mama laughed. But she gave the ragman back his ten cents,

and he gave her back the bike, and off he went with his bells tinkling in the breeze and his singsong voice chanting, "Cash paid for rags . . . cash paid for rags . . ."

Mama apologized. "I'm sorry," she said.

"Bikey is for the museum we are making our barn into," Jane explained so that Mama would not feel guilty. "You didn't know about it. Neither did Rufus and Joey until now. Bikey is going to be one of the most important things in the museum!"

Mama came around the house, paused on the back stoop, looked at the barn, and said, "A good idea! A very good idea! "I'm glad you rescued Bikey . . . a fine artifact!"

"What's an artifact, Mama?" Rufus demanded.

"Oh, things, just . . . things," said Mama as she went inside.

At first Rufus was going to put Bikey right inside the barn, but Jane stopped him. "We have to pull the sleigh out to make room for all the other things we'll be adding to the collection. Hide Bikey way back in his raspberry garage where he will be safe. He's an artifact now."

This famous bike! Every member of the family beginning with Sylvie, the real owner . . . a Christmas present when she was ten . . . then Joey, then Jane, and finally Rufus, had learned how to ride on it!

Even Mama herself had once ridden old Bikey down the narrow walk leading from the front porch to the street to see if she could still ride a bicycle! Although it was not the kind that she had learned on, with a big wheel in front and a small one behind, nevertheless she rode it from the porch to the street and did not once let it wobble onto the lawn, nor did she once fall off! The children were proud. One wheel bent, one tire flat, yet Mama rode it!

Well, Bikey was saved! Now to get on with the museum! Sleigh next. Out it had to come to be an outside museum attraction. "People will spot the sleigh," said Joey, "and say, 'Oh-ho! Here is The Moffat Museum!'"

Even though the sleigh was not a Moffat sleigh, it didn't matter. At one time or another, all of them had sat in it, Rufus the most often. He'd take the crumbling leather reins in his hands and say, "Giddy-yap! Giddy-yap!" to an imaginary pony, wish that a real pony, even an old one, had also been left behind by this sleigh's former owner. Catherine-the-cat liked this old sleigh, too. It was a place to get away from them all, to curl up on the seat, listen for a bird, or take a long snooze inside the rounded front of the sleigh . . . hidden. So of course this sleigh should be part of the museum!

Now then, to get the sleigh out!

"Let's get going!" said Rufus. "People can sit in the sleigh waiting for their turn to go into the museum. I like this museum plan, Jane."

Jane smiled.

Joey got a long piece of strong clothesline from the back entry. He tied it around Rufus's waist. Joey and Jane pushed. Rufus pulled. At last the sleigh began to budge!

"Been in here a long time," said Rufus, puffing and red in the face. "Circa one hundred years maybe. Now I'm its pony! Neigh!" he said.

All of a sudden the sleigh got going. Out it went! It slid

down the slight wooden slope at the door and was now out in the open air! They settled it at a good angle near Mrs. Price's honeysuckle vines. Anyone sitting in it could see who was coming and also overhear the comments of visitors inside.

There would be visitors, of course. News gets around.

The sleigh had cobwebs in its corners. They dusted it; they rubbed it with stove polish. You could see yourself reflected in it. Also, now you could see the fine line of golden filigree that wound around the sleigh. It was pretty!

Jane said, "When people come . . . *if* people, friends of friends, come . . . someone should always sit in the sleigh and keep order from up there. You know how people are! Even in church. Push, shove to get the prettiest geranium on Easter Sunday? Disgustin'!"

"I'll be the person that sits," said Rufus happily. He climbed into the sleigh and sat. He held the crumbling leather reins in his suntanned little fists. "Ho-ho! 'Over the hills we go . . .' " he sang. "Goes fine for a 'circa' 1800 sleigh."

"Where did you get that 'circa' business?" asked Jane.

"From Mama," said Rufus. "And she should know! Grew up in New York, where they have museum after museum after museum . . . all sorts. Well, Mama said if the people who run a museum don't know the exact date of something or other, they say 'circa' this or 'circa' that. Too lazy to go into a library, ask the library lady, or even go down into its cellar themselves, where they keep ancient books, and search for the real date. 'Circa' covers everything."

"I like an exact date, if possible," said Joey. He crawled under the sleigh to see if the creator of this fine old sleigh may have signed it: "Made by so and so . . ." and have given an exact date. But he wriggled himself out and reluctantly put in his little notebook: The Moffat Museum sleigh, circa 19th century.

This was a new little notebook he had just bought. He labeled it The Moffat Museum, commenced on this day, June 14, 1919. "No 'circa' about this fact," he said. "And no need to run down into cellars of libraries to look it up!"

"I like circa better anyway," said Rufus. "When we are dead and gone," he mused happily, "and people are excavating in Cranbury, they will come upon this museum. And they will put in their books, 'An ancient museum named Moffat, circa twentieth century.' "

"Circa early twentieth century," Jane ventured to say. "But when we put the art and other 'first' things inside, don't put circa on everything," she pleaded. "Ignorant people, even friends of friends, who don't know Latin, might think it stands for 'circus' and ask, 'Where are the clowns? The acrobats on the high trapeze?' "

"The tigers? The lions? An elephant?" Rufus added.

They all laughed. "But anyway," said Jane, "it's time to get on with placing other things besides Bikey inside."

"Just one thing more this circa nineteenth century sleigh needs," said Rufus, "is a lap robe for me to sling over my legs in cold weather, ten below . . . A blizzard maybe," he added.

"Oh, I have it! I have it!" said Jane. "Stay still, Rufus! Still as a statue! I'll be right back!"

Jane ran indoors and grabbed a little rag rug she had crocheted one summer. She had meant it to be put on the floor to keep Mama's feet warm. But the rug was too humped up in the middle and never did flatten down, so it stayed on the brown corduroy Morris chair in the dining room. Catherine-the-cat loved it because it was close to Mama, the only person in the whole world she really loved.

Now Jane tucked the rug in the rounded front part of the sleigh. There it stayed.

Next, they swept the barn. Jane wouldn't go in until she was sure that no spiders or centipedes were creeping around. Now, Bikey, of course, the first of all first things, went in, and they leaned him against the wall near the front, where he probably would be the first of all firsts to be seen.

On the ledge that wound around the barn halfway up the wall, they put many other things: a conch shell, huge with a lovely pink inside, in which you could hear the ocean roaring if you held it close to your ear; Indian arrowheads found up on West Rock near Judge's Cave; then rocks that Joey had collected that had mica on them; and next some flat cases, covered with glass, with insects mounted on pins inside them. One was named *Musca domestica.* "Ordinary flies," said Rufus. "You see how you have to know Latin to know anything!" Miss Nellie Buckle had given these to the Moffats. They liked them but kept them in the cellar so Catherine would not sit on them and study the flies in there and, clawing, break the glass.

Joey labeled everything. The way he could print! But he didn't have to print any card for the next thing. Rufus had dragged out from his raspberry garage an old friend of his. This was a cardboard Uneeda Biscuit boy in a yellow slicker, faded, true, but still holding out his hand, offering a biscuit. This figure had been on the back of Rufus's bike on many trips. He was a friend. They placed him near the front of the museum, on the left, near Bikey. He seemed to be welcoming people.

They worked fast because Joey had a certain idea in his mind, and he wanted these inside "first things" put in in a hurry. He had told them about one famous museum in Washington, where, besides the first locomotive and the first airplane, there were lots of clothes worn by famous ladies of the past. He hadn't liked this part of the museum and wanted to get on to the first steamboat.

But Jane said some people like famous old clothes even if he didn't. She asked Mama if they could have the little black trunk that was down in the cellar of the house. It was filled with famous old costumes from one play or another: a king, a prince, a firefly dress with little gold bells sewn around the bottom. Mama said they could exhibit it, that it was good to have it aired out. This they did and put it, open, in the back of the museum.

"Look! Look, look!" said Jane when they reached the bottom of the trunk. "The heads of The Three Bears!" All of them had been in that play. Joey tried on his head because he had been the Papa Bear. "Gr-r-r!" he said and made Jane and Rufus laugh. Then he tacked the heads on the wall above the trunk, and they looked very funny there. People would laugh. So, after all, the "first" old clothes section was a success. Even Joey agreed.

Jane looked around the museum then. "You know what's the matter here?" she said. "No real art! No real paintings or statues!"

Rufus objected. "The cardboard boy is art. He is a cardboard statue."

Jane laughed. "Right!" she said. "But I mean a hard statue or a painting. Real art . . . !"

Then Rufus said, "A coincidents!"

Sylvie was coming singing up the walk, and she was the artist of the family. Suddenly she stopped her singing between a tra and a la, and the children saw Sylvie and their neighbor Mrs. Price in earnest conversation. The children went closer and listened.

"Here it is!" said Mrs. Price. She handed an artist's bamboo easel over the hedge to Sylvie. It was not a toy; it was a real big easel. Moreover, on its ledge was a canvas, empty, inviting someone to paint something on it, a cow in a pasture perhaps . . . anything.

Sylvie was ecstatic. "Thank you! Thank you!" she exclaimed and would have rushed indoors with her gift, but had to listen to a little explaining, which Rufus and Jane and Joey were now near enough to hear also.

Mrs. Price said, "I was in my attic, poking around. You should see my attic some day . . . if you're not afraid of bats, that is. I spotted this easel over there in a dark corner. Wilfred, my husband, used to paint. But he hasn't for years . . . lost the knack. So I said to myself, 'One of those Moffats next door must paint, or would, if they had an easel in the house!' " Then Mrs. Price went into her own house.

The children rushed to Sylvie. They grabbed her and the easel. In a few moments they told her about The Moffat Museum and about the need for art. Sylvie understood; she left the easel for the others to set up, ran indoors, and came back in about fifteen minutes with a painting of a red fox with a bushy tail.

The children had placed the easel near the front of the museum. Now they placed the fox painting on it. It was the best place in the whole museum for the picture, because when the sun was shining, as it was now, it would shine on that big, bushy red tail. It brightened everything up and looked lovely. Then Sylvie ran away; she had so many things to do to get ready for her wedding at the end of June to the Reverend Mr. Ray Abbot!

So now there was art in the museum. While Joey was making the sign, ART, Jane remembered another thing she had for this section. She flew upstairs to her room, but came down carefully carrying a miniature art gallery she had made out of a wooden orange crate. Rufus had brought this home from the grocery store. It had been pitched out, thrown away. "People throw away the best things!" he had thought. "This is good for something."

It had been good for something all right. Jane had turned it upright and transformed it into a two-storied little art gallery.

She made tiny easels out of matchsticks and flour and water paste. Then she painted little pictures to put on each one of them. Best of all, long ago Mama had given her two little oriental rugs that had come with the boxes of Velvet tobacco Papa used to smoke in his pipes. Jane put one on each floor. They still smelled of tobacco. The boys liked the little gallery.

"Smell!" she said to them. "Smell of tobacco?"

They smelled. "Right!" they said.

Jane went outside, stood a few feet away from the museum and studied it from every angle, bending this way and that, the way an artist studies his painting. She said, "Pretend it isn't *our* museum, that it is someone else's or some famous one in some big city! Or . . . pretend you're on a guided tour like, for instance, the one led by Mr. Pennypepper, the superintendent of schools, that he has once a year. Why! It will be this very Saturday! Well . . . pretend that the thought pops into his head on this week's tour: 'Well now, what do you know? There's a museum here. Let's investigate!' "

"Criminenty!" said Rufus. The way Jane spoke, you'd think that what she was imagining was real! He tore to the street. "Not coming yet!" he reported.

Jane laughed. "I said I was just pretending. Anyway, how did it strike you . . . The Moffat Museum . . . from out there?"

"I don't need to pretend I'm somebody else, or have to galavant to the street to know what's wrong with this museum," said Joey. "It needs science! Astronomy! A meteor! One of the first things you see when you go inside a great museum in New York is a beautiful meteor . . . only they call it meteorite. And guess where we can find one of those?"

"In the Brick Lot on New Dollar Street!" Rufus and Jane said together. "Two of them side by side!"

"I'm going to keep on calling them meteors," Rufus said. "We always called them 'meteors.' Why change?"

"Right," said Joey.

"They'll be awfully heavy, and they're big!" said Jane.

"I'll get my old express wagon and string it up behind my other better one," Rufus said.

"Yeh," said Joey, laughing. "A freight train of wagons with a mighty meteor stretching from front of wagon one to back of wagon two."

"And we won't be greedy," said Jane. "Just take one. Other kids like to sit on them. I know the Pyes do. So we'll leave one behind for them to sit on and think and wonder . . ."

"We'll put our meteor outside, opposite the sleigh, on the other side of the museum," said Joey. He was very excited at the thought of this meteor.

His eagerness was catching. "Yes!" said Jane. "People coming here, after having seen the sights inside, can sit on it, rest, eat an apple. But remember, they'll be allowed to eat only outside, on the meteor section of the museum."

". . . and not be allowed to stick chewing gum on this meteor that fell on New Dollar Street circa . . . hm-m," said Rufus. "And not chip their initials into it! Nor paint hearts and arrows on it . . . nothing!"

"Maybe," mused Jane, "some people, some older people, will come at night. Maybe big people with telescopes, look for shooting stars, and let us take a turn at looking. Nice people would let us," she said.

The expedition was ready now to set forth, the two wagons knotted together with more of the old clothesline.

They went down Ashbellows Place to Elm Street, where they turned right and were soon nearing New Dollar Street, their old beloved street, where the Yellow House was in which they used to live. They were very happy.

Then, when they were very close to the córner of New Dollar Street, a terrific sound like an explosion stopped them in their tracks. Jane covered her ears and looked up at the sky. Not thunder! The sky was as blue as the dress she had on. Not a cloud!

"Wowie!" said Rufus. "A giant firecracker, and it's not even the Fourth of July!"

"Or," said Jane, recovering from her fright, "could it be that another meteor has fallen on New Dollar Street!"

"Too much of a coincidents!" said Rufus, and the three of them, cautious but curious, continued to the corner of New Dollar Street. There, however, a road block had been placed, and they could not enter. Then another terrific blast rent the air. Boom! Boom! Boom!

"I told you it might be another meteor," said Jane. "They would not fall to the earth silently."

"Naw!" said Joey. He had a look of grave misgiving on his face.

A man came along, took away the road-block wooden horse, slung it over his shoulder, and went back down New Dollar Street.

The children followed him slowly. Their spirits revived a little, though, for now they were going past the picket fence in front of the Yellow House. They looked at it fondly. Next would be the Brick Lot. But where was the Brick Lot? Where the meteors?

No one said a word.

In front of where the Brick Lot used to be, men were driving a team of oxen up from a deep hole in the ground and dumping what they had dug up into three green carts in order to take it all away. Dirt, pulverized bricks, weeds, and roots were all jumbled together. No sign of the mighty meteors!

Stunned, Jane and Rufus and Joey walked as close as possible to the fence beside the Yellow House, careful not to slide down into the deep hole where the men and their oxen were. Now they were at the place where the meteors used to be. Nothing there now but rectangular spots where the blasts they had heard had done their work.

Some beetles, upside down, were frantically trying to get themselves right side up and were thrashing their thin legs in desperation.

"Poor things!" said Rufus. He, and even Jane, helped them to right themselves. Hard black beetles were one sort of insect that Jane was not afraid of. Now, right side up, they scurried away in bewilderment.

Then Joey and Jane and Rufus hoisted themselves up onto the high wooden fence. They sat in the shade of a huge apple tree that grew in the backyard of the Yellow House and watched the proceedings in the old Brick Lot. Load after load of dirt and battered bricks were hauled up by the patient oxen, and the hole was becoming deeper and wider.

Jane said to Joey, who was the most depressed of the three of them, "Joey, maybe those meteors are in one of the carts, and all that blasting we heard was just for ordinary old bricks. I'll ask," she said.

She jumped down and cautiously went to the edge of the

hole where, down below, a man and his team of oxen were working. Clinging to a tough weed, Jane shouted, "Man! Hey! Man with oxen! What happened to the meteors? Are you an ark-yologist taking our meteors to a museum?"

"Archaeologist? Meteors? Museums? Naw! I'm just an ordinary man digging a cellar for a new house," he said.

He was a big man. His dark red shirt, turned rusty from the sun, clung to him, wet with perspiration.

The oxen rolled their red eyes at Jane. She backed away quickly and joined her brothers on the high fence.

"The meteors! The meteors!" Jane persisted. She cupped her mouth with her hands. "What did you and your oxen do with those two big meteors that have always been right down there below us. See the beetles running? There! That's where!"

Rufus chimed in, "Yes, mister. We need those meteors for *our* museum. You take one. We take the other. For science! Fair?"

"My gosh!" said the man. "Science!" He was clearly interested. You'd have thought that this was the Yukon and that he might have struck gold!

He looked in his long curved scoop. Just dirt and broken bricks. He looked back up at the Moffats. "You mean those two big hunks of stone that were over there? We didn't know they were meteors. We had to blow them to bits, kids. Too big for my carts and for our team to cart away. But if we'd'a known they were meteors, we'd never have pulverized 'em. We'd have asked the boss, Mr. J. B. Bombergh, what to do with them."

"They were great big pieces of a star in the sky that fell here long ago," said Jane sadly.

"We think," added Joey.

The big man seemed depressed. He mopped his forehead. "We never were told either to knock meteors to bits or not knock meteors to bits." Then a hopeful look spread over his face. "Busted-to-bits meteors are *star dust*. Right? Better star dust than nothing, right? There's a heap o' that in cart number three, empty so far, except for the blown-to-bits meteors. Right?"

The children jumped down and ran to green cart three. This cart did have mounds of pulverized stone, reddish, in it . . . all that was left to be seen now of their beloved old meteors.

The man followed them to the cart. "This!" he said.

In the reddish dust there were a few rather large chunks. Joey now spoke. "Wowie!" he said. "Star dust! You know that star dust might be better for our museum than the big meteor we were going to put outside at the entrance? We can put the star dust inside. Some museums may not have even a speck of star dust!"

"Well, we will!" said Rufus. "If the man lets us!"

"Star dust, eh?" said the man. He scooped some up and studied it in the palm of his hand. He looked up at the sky, though of course it was too early for even Venus to be seen. He put some in his back pocket. If it turned out to be star dust, he wanted a bit himself to take home to his wife and children. He looked at the sky again, and he smiled.

Jane and Joey and Rufus waited tensely. Then, with a wide smile, the man said, "Help yourselves!" he said. "Take as much as you like, the entire kit and caboodle!" Then he went back down into the big hole where his oxen, as motionless as statues, waited.

"What generosity!" exclaimed Jane. The three children readjusted their thoughts from mighty meteors to precious star dust. They piled a heap of this in wagon one. Rufus put one small chunk in the pocket of his khaki shorts to show and maybe *give* to Uncle Bennie Pye. Then they started for home.

"Joey!" Jane said. "Think how exciting it will be for people to see a sign over the science section . . . the part that has mica . . . that will say, STAR DUST THAT FELL ON NEW DOLLAR STREET, circa . . ."

"Circa unknown . . ." said Rufus with a laugh.

Joey laughed, too. "Yes," he said. "Fine. Fine! Yes . . ." He paused. "But I did, still sorta do, have my mind set on a big one like you see in The Museum of Natural History."

Pondering all these things . . . was the big one better, was the star dust better. . . . they continued on the way home. The way home led them past the printing press of the *Cranbury Chronicle*. They stopped here for a minute to rest and to breathe in the wonderful smell of freshly printed newspaper.

They liked the man, Mr. Peter G. Gilligan, who ran the newspaper single-handed . . . wrote it, printed it, did everything. Sometimes he gave them a long sheet, rolled up, of shiny white paper, the width of a column in his newspaper. They liked this paper, drew cartoons on it and funny-paper pictures . . .

While they were resting there, all three sitting in one or the other of the wagons, Mr. Gilligan came outdoors to cool off and have a smoke. He surveyed the star-dust express. After lighting up, puffing in and puffing out, he got the pipe going and said, "Hello, Moffats. What are you doing with all that dirt?"

"Dirt!" echoed Rufus. "Dirt! This is *star dust*! Not *dirt*!"

Jane said indignantly, "This star dust is for the 'science' section of our museum. Lead on, Joey! We have work to do!"

"Wait!" said Mr. Gilligan, knocking and emptying his pipe against the wall. "Museum! What museum?"

"*Our* museum," said Jane. "The Moffat Museum! It is the

barn in our backyard. The museum will be free and will have things in it important to us Moffats. Like this star dust . . ."

"Hm-m-m," said Mr. Gilligan. "S'wonder any news at all gets into the *Cranbury Chronicle* . . . nobody telling me anything . . ." He rushed back into his printing shop, muttering, "Just in time to get this in the early edition!"

He was in such a hurry that he didn't even think to give the children one single roll of the shiny paper. They heard the press go up and come down. They stood waiting for a few minutes. "No shiny paper today," Rufus said. "Pooh!"

Then they trudged on. When they reached home, they put the star dust in a shoe box labeled Enna Jettick. Joey made a sign to paste over this. His sign said: STAR DUST THAT FELL IN THE BRICK LOT ON NEW DOLLAR STREET NEXT TO THE YEL-LOW HOUSE.

"You forgot 'circa,' " said Rufus.

Joey laughed. But he added, " 'Circa unknown.' "

They were tired. "Made a whole museum in half a day," said Jane.

"A museum is never finished," said Joey.

Then they all started to go into the house. They looked back at the museum. "Maybe every day . . . perhaps even tomorrow . . . something new will pop into our heads," said Jane. "Something just right for the museum."

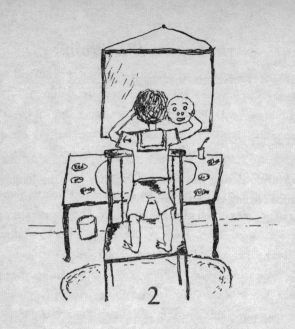

2

THE PENNYPEPPER TOUR

THE NEXT AFTERNOON AT SCHOOL IT WAS RUFUS'S TURN
to erase the blackboard and to clap the erasers. While he was
doing this cherished job, an idea clapped its way into his head,
and he began to mull it over. The more he mulled, the funnier
it became. It fitted right in with the way things were going at
home, right in with the plans for The Moffat Museum.

He was going to be a waxworks statue, art and statues being
what were most needed in the museum.

"How'd I ever get that idea?" he asked himself. "Easy enough," he answered himself as he clapped away. "This is how."

After the geography lesson, the teacher, Miss Miles, had asked the question she asked her class every year. "What are you going to do during this summer vacation . . . the long, long vacation coming very soon now?"

Most answered, "Nothing." But one or two said they were going to visit an aunt or a grandfather somewhere. One was going to a camp in Maine for two weeks. One boy said he was going to Fire Island, where he had been once before. That sounded next best to nothing, Rufus thought. "Nothing" was a huge hole you could fill up with anything. He did not say one thing to Miss Miles about The Moffat Museum, which would fill up a great deal of that big hole meaning nothing on his vacation. He didn't want all the kids in this class following him home to take a look.

Then Miss Miles had told the class what she was going to do. She was going to London, England. One thing she was planning to do there, besides see London Bridge, was to visit Madame Tussaud's Waxworks Museum. "Filled," she said, "with wax statues of famous people, some famous dead people, some famous live people." She wrote the name on the blackboard. "You pronounce it Tusso," she said.

That was the first time Rufus had heard of a museum like that. As he erased the large letters spelling Madame Tussaud's Waxworks Museum, the words stuck in his mind. When he was clapping the erasers out the window, squinting his eyes together not to get chalk dust in them and trying not to breathe more than necessary, the idea of his being a waxworks statue came into his head. Rufus, the waxworks boy! It struck him funny, Rufus, a famous waxworks statue, in The Moffat Museum. He couldn't help laughing out loud.

Giving the erasers one last clap, he turned around, still laughing, his hair white with chalk dust. Who should come walking into the room then but Mr. Pennypepper, the superintendent of schools. He handed Miss Miles a note, saw Rufus, and observed, "Gray, before his time, and hoary." Then he left.

Rufus liked that . . . gray before his time . . . hoary. . . . It helped him to enlarge upon his waxworks idea. Gray, hoary hair, frost, light snow having fallen on this waxworks statue, him, sitting in the sleigh.

He put the erasers on the ledge, said, "Good-by, Miss Miles," and before she could ask him what was so funny, he tore out of the school and home.

"Mama!" said Rufus. "You ever hear of a waxworks museum?"

"Yes," said Mama. "There's a famous one in London . . . Madame Tussaud's Waxworks Museum."

"True," said Rufus. "And you pronounced it right. Tusso!"

Rufus went outdoors, sat on the back stoop, and ate a bread-and-apple-butter sandwich. He studied the museum with the sleigh in front, all polished up, pretty black sleigh with filigrees just waiting for someone to sit in it . . . him, Rufus Moffat, a waxworks boy, sitting in the sleigh, holding on the reins, not moving. "What a great addition to the artifacts!" he thought. "More interesting than famous dresses, easels, and such."

"Look!" people would say. "Besides being the one and only museum in Cranbury, it has a waxworks statue in it. Can any museum you know of beat that?"

Wait till Jane and Joey heard this and *saw* this! He didn't know where they were, gone off somewhere, maybe on some artifact-finding expedition. He'd get busy right away with his transformation . . . not wait for them. Nice to surprise them anyway . . .

He went indoors, moved from room to room, and collected all the wax crayons, bits of candles, the wax Mama rubbed her flat iron on to make it smooth . . . he had to peel the scorched cloth off that . . . even little half-burnt birthday candles being saved for another cake probably. He found some jars of home-made strawberry jelly covered with wax that Mama had stored on the top shelf of the pantry. He carefully took the white wax off the tops of these. He did not dip his fingers into the jelly, just licked the wax tops, then covered the open jars with paper so ants would not get in, or bees. What a collection of wax he had from here or there!

He thought he had enough to transform himself into a waxworks boy. He put some saucers on the kitchen table to keep the colors separate. Not being allowed to light matches, he asked Mama if she would help him melt wax.

Mama said, "All right. But what's all this for?" Mama shrugged and melted the wax. "What for?" she repeated.

"You'll see, Mama. You'll see!" said Rufus.

Then the doorbell rang. It was Mrs. Shoemaker, come to try on her new dress. She was one of the ladies for whom Mama, the best dressmaker in Cranbury, sewed. So Mama left and did not witness the transformation of Rufus into a waxworks boy statue.

Rufus put the saucers on the sink, over which there was a small square mirror. He got a chair and watched as he made himself into a Madame Tussaud waxworks statue.

He patted the wax on his face, dark pink cheeks, blues and purples for shadows, here and there white on his hoary forehead, some red on his nose. He figured if he were sitting in a sleigh, his nose would be red . . . it would be wintertime. Hav-

ing it wintertime made the whole undertaking easier. All he'd
have to make out of wax was his face, a mask. He could wear
mittens, a woolen cap pulled down to meet the collar of his old
plaid mackinaw, and a scarf around his neck. He could stiffen
the mittens a little bit with wax and maybe put some white wax
on his cap. The rest of him would be covered by the humped-up-
in-the-middle rag rug Jane had crocheted. No one would sus-
pect that he was bare-kneed.

This would all make a winter scene, waxworks boy Rufus,
holding reins in an antique sleigh on a cold and frosty day . . .
a hoary day!

Being a fast worker, it didn't take Rufus long to do all of
this. It hurt only a little when he took his wax face off his real
face. He had left small holes for his eyes, for his nostrils, and a
wide hole for his mouth. The eye holes were so small that no
one could possibly see his eyes if he blinked. He would practice, without his waxworks uniform on, sitting immobile in the
sleigh, being a Madame Tussaud statue, so when the time came
to be an artifact, he would be a perfect waxworks one.

He then carefully laid his face on a newspaper . . . an old
issue of the *Cranbury Chronicle* . . . on a shelf inside the cellar
door. He dug around in closets upstairs and downstairs for
mittens, scarf, woolen cap, and last year's mackinaw, put the
last of his wax on these, and put everything together on the

deep shelf beside his face. It was always cool in the cellar, and his face would not melt. As he was about to leave his treasures, his eyes were caught by the page in the *Cranbury Chronicle* open to the "What's New in Cranbury" section.

"A coincidents," he said to himself.

This week's *Chronicle* would be out today.

He went outdoors, pleased with what he had done. He got up in the sleigh and sat there to rest, but there wasn't time for that. Riding around the side of the house came Joey with Jane on the crossbar. They were very excited. They had a copy of the *Cranbury Chronicle*, so hot off the press that ink came off on their hands.

Jane hopped down. "Look at this, Rufus, look!"

"Just take a look at this!" echoed Joey. They handed Rufus the newspaper. Rufus looked. There on the page that had the column "What's New in Cranbury" was . . .

"Read it out loud," Jane implored.

Rufus read:

"At last! A museum in Cranbury! Unlike any of our neighboring towns and hamlets, Cranbury alone now has a museum. It is a special museum and is named The Moffat Museum. It is situated in the yard of the Moffats' house at 12 Ashbellows Place, easy to get to, right off the trolley line. There will be no charge for admission. Like the *Cranbury Chronicle*, it is *free!*"

"O-o-oh! People will come!" gasped Jane. "They might be on their way now, on foot, in trolleys, by horse and wagon, in a car . . ."

"And you know what," said Joey gloomily. "Tomorrow is the day Mr. Pennypepper takes a group of children, who want to join in, on a visit to important places in Cranbury. It is the day of the Pennypepper tour."

"Ts!" Jane gasped again. In her fancies, when she had thought up the museum, the idea of people coming to it seemed like fun. But now with that possibility perhaps coming true, she trembled. "Supposing Mr. Pennypepper and all of them come?" she asked.

Tomorrow was Saturday. Mr. Pennypepper always conducted this tour on a Saturday, so the boys and girls would not miss one single important lesson in arithmetic, geography, anything. "Every second counts in your schooling," he reminded them all. And he said, "Meet me on the front steps of Union School tomorrow morning at nine o'clock on the dot. No chewing gum. The tour is to places renowned for their dignity."

"Lucky it's not today," said Rufus. "I'm not quite ready. But why be such gloomy guts?"

"We're gloomy because when Mr. Pennypepper reads the

paper and sees the 'What's New in Cranbury' page . . . 'At last!
A museum in Cranbury!' and all the rest of it . . . he might
squeeze our museum into his tour," said Joey crossly. "That's
why we're gloomy."

"The Superintendent of Schools! Mr. Pennypepper stopping
here on his tour, that's what scares us," said Jane. "I'm afraid
of him . . . such an important man! Kids, yes. Superintendents
of schools, no!"

Rufus laughed. "Let him come; oh, let them come! They'll
get a real surprise." And he went in to see how his waxworks
face was doing cooling in the cellarway.

This annual tour was supposed to be a lot of fun, on the
order of a Sunday School picnic, except there was never anything to eat at the famous stops. No swimming or egg races
either.

"Isn't the tour always the same?" asked Jane. "Like the time
I went on it?"

"Just about always the same," said Joey. "There are four
stopping places, and they stick to these mainly . . . only stop
once in a while if some kid, say, sees a rare bird. Then Mr.
Pennypepper gets out his little bird book and looks it up."

"We're not a little thing," said Rufus, who, satisfied that his
face was hardening in the cellar, had rejoined the others.

"No, we're not a little thing, like a bird. We're a whole

museum," said Jane sadly. "I'm really scared that the great Mr. Pennypepper might come here on his tour."

"What are the four regular stops?" asked Rufus.

Joey got out his little notebook to remind himself of the usual stops, just four, on the Tour of Important Places held each year by Pop Pennypepper. This was an affectionate nickname for the Superintendent of Schools, who was liked and respected.

"If they come, don't forget and call him Pop," Rufus interrupted.

"Nope," said Joey. "Here we go then."

"*Stop Number One*: The public Library, where the librarian shows this and that but especially the big dictionary. 'How many pages in that book?' some kid always asks.

" 'Three thousand and two hundred and ten,' the librarian says. She doesn't even have to look it up. She knows it by heart. Some kids believe her but want to see for themselves. So the librarian lets them look. True! The kid who asked the question pretends to faint. Like dominoes, all the kids follow suit. Mr. Pennypepper says, 'Get up, children. Children, get up. More sights to be seen.' As we leave, some kids keep repeating the number of pages in the big dictionary so they can tell their mothers and fathers. 'There are 3,210! Don't believe me? Go and see!'

"Then we go out of the library. Most kids circle the two tall lamps on each side of the top of the steps before they go down. 'The granite is from the quarries of Rockport, Massachusetts,' Mr. Pennypepper says as we go down on our way to:

"*Stop Number Two*: This is the printing press of the *Cranbury Chronicle*, run by Mr. Peter G. Gilligan. When we go in, he tells us it had been run by his father before him, and *his* father before *him*! All the kids like this place. It's the only stop where the kids are given something to take home. Nothing to eat, but nice strips of shiny paper, the width of a column in the *Chronicle*. 'For galleys,' Mr. Gilligan tells us. 'Nothing to do with ancient boats.' He lets one or two of the kids press down on the narrow galleys and see 'What's New in Cranbury' come out on the paper. All the kids crowd around to see what they had made the press print. And everybody learns to count the picas (not a strange pie—a word for 'type') and figure how many would fit on a line. The kids, even me, want to be printers when we grow up. We like this place, don't want to leave. But we like the next one, too.

"*Stop Number Three*: This is a visit to the front porch of Mr. Buckle, the oldest inhabitant of Cranbury, one hundred and two years old on his last birthday! The kids love to visit him. He has a glass cabinet filled with furniture that he made out of chicken bones . . . tiny, tiny chairs, tables, a sofa, beds, and a grandfather clock. He makes the clock go tick-tock, tick-tock with his veined and frail old hands.

"On visiting day he has the cabinet moved out onto the front porch. He sits beside it in a rocker and rocks as he makes the clock go tick-tock and answers questions not only about the furniture but about his long life in the Army. Then the kids file down the steps. 'Thank you, Mr. Buckle, thank you!' they say. And to each other say, 'Did you hear the grandfather clock go tick-tock and hear its little bell?'

"*Stop Number Four*: A visit to the oldest house in Cranbury built in colonial times. The fireplace is so big you can stand in it. Most kids do, if they have the chance. And the girls set the little cradle by the big bed rocking, rocking. Then, after this stop, it's back to the steps of Union School where we are to be dismissed. Mr. Pennypepper's final words are, 'Good-by to you all. You have learned a great deal . . . use your wisdom wisely,' he says and smiles. Most kids don't hear him, they're so hungry, and they tear off, starving for lunch! I wait to hear him, though. Seems polite. So does the teacher. Then Mr. Pennypepper tips his hat to her, and he goes his way and she hers. And I, mine. Here!

"End of annual tour."

When Joey concluded his record of the Pennypepper tour as it was usually conducted, he closed his little black notebook, put an elastic band around it, and slipped it into his back pocket. The tour, even in Joey's fine handwriting, took up almost the entire notebook.

Jane was enthralled by his tale of a usual tour. "Joey should be a writer," she thought. Then, remembering the tour would not even gather until tomorrow on the steps of Union School, Jane said, "I'm not going to be gloomy. Don't you look so gloomy, Joey."

"You should be gloomy, too," said Joey. "The tour might change its course. Stop Number Three might be The Moffat Museum before the chicken-bone furniture! We live on the same street as Mr. Buckle, don't we? Our house is reached before his because our house is number twelve and his is twenty-one. They might swing in here after the press and before the furniture! I just don't like surprises. Anyway, I need a haircut."

"Maybe I should put my hair up in rag curlers," mused Jane. "Just in case . . ." She smoothed her hair as though it were already tomorrow and the class were marching in. Then she said, "Aw! Let's forget it! Probably most people don't read the *Chronicle* anyway . . . just chuck it away because it's free."

Rufus, who had listened to all of this in silence, now spoke.

"Well, I hope Mr. Pennypepper does squeeze The Moffat Museum into the tour. Just so they don't squeeze me!" He laughed and slapped his knee and gasped, "Oh, my!"

"What's so funny? Let us in on the joke!" said Jane, laughing in spite of not knowing.

For a moment Rufus was tempted to tell Jane and Joey about his plan to make himself into a museum piece, a waxworks boy statue such as they have in London at Madame Tussaud's. Then he thought he shouldn't. If the Pennypepper tourists did come tomorrow and Jane and Joey were struck dumb, turned to stone themselves, the sight of him might stir them into life. There he would be, sitting in winter attire in the sleigh, a Madame Tussaud statue. Joey and Jane would be so relieved, not be nervous any more. They would be able to say, "Star dust," or "Heads of The Three Bears," when the people went inside the museum. So he said nothing.

However, their anxiety did have some effect on him. He went into the kitchen to have a private waxworks boy rehearsal. His mask had hardened nicely. No one was around. First he put on his last winter's frayed plaid mackinaw, then his mask. Then he tied a scarf around his neck, covering slightly the chin of his mask. Then he pulled on his old red woolen cap, which covered the place where mask left off and real head began, and finally his mittens stiff with wax.

He went into the living room and sat down in the green velvet Morris chair, which he pretended was the sleigh. He could imagine what he looked like sitting there. He held imaginary reins in his stiff hands. He could see through the little eye holes. He practiced not moving his eyes to right or left. He could breathe through the two little holes for his nose and the one for his mouth. Even though he could stick his tongue out, he would not do so even if Letitia Murdock stuck hers out. Even if someone stuck a pin in him, he would not say, "Ouch!" Just remember every second he was a statue and made of wax!

"Phew!" he said. "It's hot!"

He took off his waxworks artifacts, put them back on the shelf in the cellarway, and then did what he had forgotten to do so far. He made a sign: RUFUS, THE WAXWORKS BOY. Joey usually made the signs. He had made a big one and nailed it on the frame of the doorway high up on the barn. It said: THE MOFFAT MUSEUM. But Rufus did the best he could and stored it with his other artifacts. He was all prepared for the visitation should it come.

After supper he and Jane and Joey sat on the front stoop. It was a lovely evening. They watched the last rosy glow of the sunset spreading over the sky beyond the library. The evening star appeared faintly in the darkening sky.

"That's Venus," said Joey.

They forgot about tomorrow. They forgot about the museum, they forgot about "What's New in Cranbury," Mr. Pennypepper, the tour. Mama came out with a pitcher of lemonade with a chunk of ice in it and some glasses. She sat down in the green wicker rocker and fanned herself with a palm-leaf fan. She told them how pretty it was on this sort of evening in Montowese, especially after a picnic on Peter's Rock.

Then Sylvie came running up, breathless. She sat down beside them. "Did you see the *Chronicle*?" she asked.

"We all saw it," said Mama calmly. "But you know what people will say if they read about your museum? They'll just say, 'How nice! We'll go there some day.' And then they'll forget all about it. Anyway," she added thoughtfully, "you may borrow the china head in case ..."

The china head was what Papa used to keep his Velvet tobacco in. Mama said it looked like Papa, but not as handsome.

Then the children walked around the museum before they went in. Even in the dusk, they thought it looked pretty. "A golden fox on an easel at this end," said Jane, "star dust at the other ..."

"And wait," thought Rufus, "till they see a waxen statue in

the sleigh!" But he didn't say anything, and soon they all went upstairs to bed.

Peace and quietude settled over the house. The last thing Jane heard as she was falling asleep was a little laugh from the boys' room. "Rufus laughing in his sleep," she thought.

3

RUFUS, THE WAXWORKS BOY

THE NEXT DAY, SATURDAY, WAS A BEAUTIFUL ONE, NOT quite as hot as the day before. Birds whistling in the trees, pigeons cooing, hens in Mrs. Price's yard cluck-clucking . . . all, all serene. Jane and Joey went down to breakfast. No sign of Rufus at the moment, but he came up out of the cellar. "Cool down there," he said.

Rufus looked at Jane and Joey. It was clear that the thoughts and fears of the Pennypepper brigade had swept over them again, that The Moffat Museum might really become Stop Three on the tour.

They looked at the clock . . . nine o'clock. The children would be gathering now on the steps of Union School in their Sunday best, preparing for the annual tour.

Jane said, "Make a sign for yourself, Joey, to pin on your shirt. Say GUARD on it, so no one will take a pinch of star dust or something. Make a sign for me. Put . . . let's see . . . put EXPLAINER on mine. I'll explain the artifacts. How's that? And make one for Rufus. Put . . . let's see . . ."

Rufus said, "Don't make a sign for me. I've already made mine."

"What's it say?" asked Jane.

"Well," said Rufus. "You'll see! Ha-ha! You'll see."

"No funny business," said Jane. "If they come, no funny business. No trying to be a ventriloquist, a talking bear, or something. Mr. Pennypepper might make you stay back, not get promoted."

Rufus didn't answer. They might be right. He resisted the temptation to tell Jane and Joey; he wanted to surprise them with his waxworks artifacts. He was the only Moffat who hoped The Moffat Museum would be Stop Three. Anyway Joey and Jane had run out to the museum to look it over. Sylvie's fox looked resplendent with the sun shining on its bushy tail. This

48

buoyed them up a little, so with their little signs pinned on them, GUARD for Joey, EXPLAINER for Jane, they then were ready for come what, come may.

Jane ran into the house, got the china head, and put it high on the ledge in the ART section.

While the coast was clear, Rufus decided to get himself into his waxworks artifacts and be ready for the Pennypepper visitation should it come. He disappeared into the cellarway, leaving the door ajar a little to get some light.

While Rufus was thus transforming himself, Jane suggested to Joey that he post himself at the front of the house, beside the porch. From here he could report the progress of the tour.

There they were, marching down Elm Street to the *Cranbury Chronicle*. So far, so good. Then, in a while, sheets of shiny paper in hand, there they were again at the corner of Ashbellows Place.

"Jane!" Joey called. "Here they are!"

Jane came running. "Where's Rufus?" she asked. "We might need him."

Enthralled by the sight of the oncoming Pennypepper tour, Jane and Joey did not see Rufus as he emerged from the cellar, all decked out in his waxworks clothes. He stuck his sign, RUFUS, THE WAXWORKS BOY, on the front of the sleigh, and settled himself comfortably in it, rag rug slung over his lap concealing his bare brown legs, crackling leather reins held awkwardly in his waxed mittens. He could see out of his two little eye holes. He could breathe, and he could stick his tongue out of the hole for his mouth if necessary. He would resist the temptation to do that, however, and remember always he was a wax statue not given to sticking out tongues. His scarf was wound snugly around his neck so you couldn't tell where wax-works face and unwaxed clothes with the real Rufus inside began.

Along came Jane, running, panting!

She stopped in her tracks at the side of the house. She gasped. The effect was terrific! "Behold Rufus, the Waxworks Boy!" Rufus muttered. "Don't say one word to me; I am *art*. These may be my last words for a long time . . ." And these were the last words he was going to say for a long time. Wax-works statues do not talk.

He smoothed the rug over his lap, enjoying the effect of all of this on Jane, who was stunned into silence.

Joey tore around the house. "They're comin'! They're comin'," he said. "They're mustering forces at the beginning of our sidewalk ready to turn in. They *have* made us Stop Three!"

Then Joey spotted Rufus. He nearly fell over Catherine-the-cat, who was looking for her rug. Jane said, "Joey! Don't say one word to Rufus. He is a Madame Tussaud waxworks statue, and those statues do not talk. Don't act surprised."

"O.K., O.K. They're comin'! They're comin'!" said Joey frantically.

"Don't run away! Get in position at the door," said Jane. "You're just the guard, remember. You don't have to say anything. But you're real . . . not waxworks, so if you think of a word, you can say it, or nod your head, or point," said Jane, determined not to get in a panic. The sight of Rufus sitting stiffly in the sleigh was reassuring.

Now, up the narrow walk that led from the street came, in stately fashion, the children of the expedition, Mr. Pennypepper in the lead, swinging his walking stick. He suggested that instead of walking two by two, they come in single file. "Do not step on the grass!" he warned.

The procession was in this order: Mr. Pennypepper, then the boys, next the girls, and finally Miss Grymes, bringing up the rear and clapping her hands softly to keep the line slowly, slowly moving, and counting the children now and then. But everybody was curious about The Moffat Museum, and no one even thought of slipping away.

Now the line had reached the front porch where Mama, speechless at the invasion, was standing in the open doorway. She had the sense to take off her big blue-checked apron and throw it behind the front door before the noted Superintendent of Schools, Mr. Eugene S. Pennypepper, held up his hand and halted the procession. She was stupefied when Mr. Penny-pepper, taking off his derby hat, asked politely, "Is this Number 12 Ashbellows Place?"

"Ah yes, Mr. Pennypepper," Mama answered.

"This then is the location of The Moffat Museum as de-scribed in the *Cranbury Chronicle* that came off the press yes-terday. We, a special group from Union School, would like to visit the museum if we may?"

Mama smiled. She leaned over the railing and mutely, hav-ing caught a glimpse of Rufus in the sleigh, nodded and pointed to the rear.

Slowly the line filed around the house.

Then there they were in a sort of two-rowed semicircle before the museum. And there they observed the Moffats in this order: Joey with a small sign pinned on him that said GUARD, standing in the doorway of the museum. Opposite him stood Jane with a small sign pinned on her blue voile dress that said EXPLAINER. But few paid attention to those two Moffats, for there, sitting in an antique sleigh, was a statue, RUFUS, THE WAXWORKS BOY. So the sign on the front of the sleigh said.

All eyes were riveted on this artifact. Now it was impossible to keep the children in any kind of line. They thronged around the sleigh. They couldn't be torn away. "What a funny thing!"

a little girl said. "Once our teacher told us about a strange museum in London where there are statues of famous people made of wax. Now we don't have to go to London to see one."

"Is Rufus a famous person?" someone asked.

No one answered.

But there were some skeptical boys and girls. Was this a waxworks statue of Rufus like one of Madame Tussaud's people? Most thought so. Or was this the real Rufus Moffat?

"Hey, Rufe!" shouted a boy standing right next to the sleigh.

But Rufus looked neither to left nor right. His eyes stared straight ahead, and he said nothing. His hands held steady on the reins, his waxworks mittens stiffly grasping them. Nothing anybody said or did affected him. He did not blink.

The children had been held spellbound by the waxworks boy. They said nothing. It was as though if anyone spoke, Rufus, the waxworks boy, might stand up and address the group, which might be spooky. But no such thing. A waxworks statue does not speak. He or she just *is*.

However, a girl named Letitia Murdock said, "What's Rufus Moffat doing up there in that old antique sleigh, that nice old antique sleigh, not explaining anything? Joey, what is your brother, Rufus Moffat, doing? Bamboozling?"

Joey replied, "I am just the guard. Do not touch the artifact, not that one or any of the ones inside."

Jane stepped forward. "I am the explainer, the guide." Jane decided to do some explaining. Otherwise, the class might hover around the sleigh forever, watching Rufus. And he might melt.

"This is Rufus, a waxworks statue. One of you has already mentioned Madame Tussaud's Museum. This is our waxworks statue part of the ART section of our museum. Now, step inside and see the rest of the artifacts . . . star dust . . . bears' heads . . ." Jane said.

But Letitia did not let her finish. She was not satisfied. In spite of Mr. Pennypepper's obvious displeasure . . . he had a way of rocking back and forth on his toes when he was displeased . . . Letitia went on anyway. "I been watchin' and watchin', and I saw the waxworks boy named Rufus blink!"

She was about to climb up on the sleigh and study Rufus more closely, and although Rufus thought he should have put a rope around the sleigh, the way they do around dinosaurs in the Peabody Museum to discourage ignoramuses from trying to touch, still he did not move a muscle or blink!

Mr. Pennypepper was quite angry with Letitia. He said firmly, "He did not blink. I have been standing in front, to the right and to the left of this waxworks statue, and it did not blink!" Silence followed this.

Mr. Pennypepper then looked at his watch. "Let those in the rear step forward and survey this remarkable artifact, and let the ones in front who have had more than ample time to study it, file slowly inside the museum and examine what's next. Remember! Do not touch an artifact!"

"The artifacts! The artifacts!" some children shouted.

Jane's heart pounded with excitement! And it pounded with elation! Thanks to Rufus, the tour so far had been an astounding success! She was proud of Rufus, who, in spite of what Letitia claimed, had not moved his eyes to right or left. The superintendent of all the schools in Cranbury had said so. That was smart of Rufus to make the holes for his eyes so small! For a little fellow who loved to run and climb and be on the go all the time, it was astounding that he had been able to sit as still as a statue all this time! And to be a winter waxworks boy on such a hot day!

Even when Catherine-the-cat, spotting all these people thronging around Rufus in the sleigh, covered by her favorite hand-crocheted rug, sprang from behind the honeysuckle, landed on Rufus's lap, and crawled under the humped-up rug, even then Rufus's hands did not tremble. His eyes stared straight ahead. Even if she had scratched him, he gave no sign.

Letitia could not resist one final remark. On her way into the museum, she said, "*If* that boy in the sleigh is not the live Rufus, if that *is* a waxworks statue of Rufus, where is the real Rufus? Let him come out from wherever he is and stand beside the sleigh!"

Jane said calmly, "This is not a hide-and-seek game where

you say, 'Come out, come out wherever you are!' This is a museum, The Moffat Museum!"

The children behind Letitia pushed her into the museum. They wanted to see the rest and shoved her aside.

They wanted to see the artifacts. "The artifacts! The artifacts! We want to see the artifacts!" more and more children shouted.

"Where are the artifacts?" demanded Letitia Murdock. "Do they fly?"

"All, all, or almost all things here are artifacts," Jane, the explainer, said with a wide sweep of her arms.

"What is an artifact?" demanded Letitia. "Do those flies on pins, when no one is looking, fly?"

Here Joey saw fit to say something. "Art is to fact what fact is to art."

Mr. Pennypepper overheard this remark and nodded his head. "An astute algebraic solution. Q.E.D.," he said sagely.

Once inside the museum, the children were impressed, although they had hoped for more waxworks. Some liked the painting of a fox on Sylvie's easel, and the star dust was a great attraction.

"What is this old thing doing here?" Letitia demanded, pointing to the old brown bike.

Jane said, "Because we all learned to ride on it!"

Letitia also wanted to know about the china head, safe high up on its shelf.

"Is that a waxworks beheaded head?" she asked.

"No," said Jane. "That is a china head of a man that my mother says looks exactly like my father. My papa used to keep his Velvet tobacco in it for his pipe."

Jane carefully took the head down. She did not let anyone touch it, but she said anyone who wanted to could smell the inside of it. There was still the faintest scent of tobacco in it. "It is the most precious thing inside the museum. I have to bring it back inside the house unless someone is here to guard it."

Some liked Jane's miniature gallery, made out of an empty wooden orange crate. She told them that the tiny oriental rugs on its two floors had come as souvenirs in the boxes of Velvet tobacco Papa used to buy and that Mama had given them to her.

Now Letitia was impressed. She poked her head close to the little art gallery. She was careful not to knock over even one little easel. She sniffed. "They do smell like the china head," she said positively. As many as could lined up to compare sniffs, of the rugs and of the head, and agreed. Many vowed that this afternoon they would go to the store and ask if there were any empty orange crates so they could make a miniature gallery, too.

Now everybody had been inside and outside The Moffat Museum. Those who did not have a barn in their backyard wished they had one and could make a museum, too. Mr. Pennypepper was standing on the far side of the sleigh in the scant shade of the honeysuckle vines. He was rocking back and forth from heel to toe, jingling coins and keys, and often surveying Rufus with an appreciative sort of smile. Even Catherine-the-cat, under her cozy little rug, did not move and could have been a waxworks museum cat.

Miss Grymes clapped her hands to gather the children into formation. Mr. Pennypepper took his gold watch out of his vest pocket. He always wore a vest, no matter how hot the day was.

"Hurry the group into line," he said to Miss Grymes. "We are off schedule because of having added another stop to our annual tour. And what a splendid addition it was, a wonder and a delight! Now we must catch up, walk fast, not to keep Mr. Buckle waiting, eager as he always is to exhibit his chicken-bone furniture, another wonder and delight for all of us. Thank you, Jane, and thank you, Joseph," and he tipped his hat to Rufus, the waxworks statue.

Joey thought he saw Mr. Pennypepper wink at Rufus.

Then Mr. Pennypepper started walking down the narrow sidewalk past the house, the line of boys following behind him, then the girls, and finally Miss Grymes, who asked Letitia to walk beside her. She thought she saw a pin in Letitia's hands and suspected, but did not know for sure, that Letitia might stick the pin into Rufus.

Mama was standing on the front porch, half hidden by the hop vines. She was worried. Should she ask them in for tea, or lemonade? She had only two lemons and not many glasses, even jelly ones. Her heart skipped a beat when Mr. Pennypepper paused in front of the porch and addressed her. Taking off his hat and bowing slightly, he said, "Mrs. Moffat. There should be a plaque on your house . . . The Moffat Museum. In smaller letters you might add, if you want, 'In the rear!' or even say, 'By appointment only!' making certain afterwards that all the artifacts are in their right places . . . the waxworks statue, for example. Children, say, 'Thank you, Mrs. Moffat.' And thank the museum workers!"

The children gathered around the front porch. They said, "Thank you, Mrs. Moffat. It was great! And thank Joey and Jane and . . ."

They turned around for one last look at the sleigh and at Rufus, the waxworks boy, in his wintry attire.

". . . and thank Rufus, the waxworks boy."

Then Rufus stood up. He waved! "Good-by!" he called. He held his arm straight out to them and stiffly waved his waxen hand. "Good-by!" he said again.

"The statue spoke! Rufus, the waxworks statue, spoke!" The children gasped. Then they burst into roars of laughter. They shouted! They clapped! They danced up and down! "Rufus! Rufus! You were great! Oh, what a wonderful waxworks statue boy you were! Hurray for Rufus Moffat, the waxworks boy!"

"The Madame Tussaud waxworks boy!" Letitia added.

Mr. Pennypepper tipped his hat, waved, and started down the street. Then many children, walking backward, went down the narrow path to the street waving and waving to Rufus, who also waved as long as he could see them.

Now Rufus stepped out of the sleigh! "Phew!" he said. He shed one artifact after another, carefully removing his wax face and laying it on his mackinaw. No longer Rufus, the waxworks boy, he stood on the seat of the sleigh, clad now only in his cool khaki shorts!

Jane said to him, "Oh, Rufus! You were the best artifact of all." She patted his bare brown knee.

And Joey said, "The best, the very best! I didn't have to say one word. Even if we had had the mighty meteor, you would still have been the best artifact in The Moffat Museum!"

4

THE FLOWER GIRL

THE HEAT WAVE HAD BROKEN. IT WAS A PERFECT SUMMER'S day, and tomorrow would be, too, if the weatherman was right. Jane was sitting on the front porch in the shade of the hop vines, thinking about tomorrow, for that was going to be Sylvie's wedding day. She was to be married at noon in the little granite church on the green.

As if that weren't enough, Jane had more to think about. She was going to be a flower girl, *the* flower girl in Sylvie's wedding. Jane had never been to a wedding, much less been in one.

Until now she had not had much time to think about what you do being a flower girl. The museum had taken up all her thinking time for many days. "I shouldda thought up the museum *after* the wedding, not before it," she mused.

People who are going to be flower girls should be told a long, long time in advance, say, a month at least, to get used to the idea, but she'd known it for only a few days. Still, you couldn't blame anyone for that. At first Sylvie and Ray Abbot were going to be married without anyone else in the wedding at all. Just the two of them and, of course, the minister. Ray wanted the wedding to be as simple as possible. Finally Sylvie persuaded Ray to let Jane be her flower girl. Now at least one other Moffat would be part of the wedding. And it would still be a "simple" wedding as Ray wished.

The sweet smell of roses, which were bursting into bloom along Mrs. Price's fence to the left of the porch, filled the air. All up and down the street, in almost everybody's garden, roses were bursting into blossom. Jane drew in a deep, long breath. Then she jumped up and plucked one pale pink rose that was drooping over the fence. She sat down again and buried her nose in it to absorb its soft, sweet fragrance.

"O-o-oh, my!" she murmured.

Jane sat there smelling and smelling her rose. She was waiting for Sylvie. Sylvie had missed the great Pennypepper day at the museum, missed the ohs! and the ahs! about her painting of a bushy-tailed fox on her easel, not seen her little brother Rufus being a Madame Tussaud waxworks boy statue.

Well, Sylvie had plenty to think about besides museums . . . showers to go to, parties, dances. Now, in a few minutes, she was about to rush home from one of these special affairs to try on her wedding dress.

Jane was waiting for her because she wanted to see how Sylvie was going to look on this last day before her wedding. She wanted to study Sylvie as she came up the walk, try to gather how she felt about becoming the Reverend Mrs. Raymond Abbot tomorrow.

Indoors, Mama was putting the finishing touches on Sylvie's wedding dress in tiny, tiny stitches, all by hand. The dress was spread like a fleecy cloud all over the dining-room table.

Fortunately, Mrs. Shoemaker's silver anniversary dress had been finished. This had given Mama just enough time to concentrate on the wedding. When Mrs. Shoemaker had walked off with her stiff taffeta silver anniversary dress held carefully over her left arm, Mama had sighed with relief. "Let's hope that is the end of that!" she said. "Let's hope she neither gains nor loses one inch until after her big celebration."

64

"I know," said Jane with sympathy. "You should put a sign on the door: NO MORE SEWING UNTIL AFTER SYLVIE'S WEDDING! We put a sign on the museum: CLOSED FOR WEDDING. And we put Rufus, I mean, waxworks boy Rufus, in the cellar to cool . . . his face anyway."

Despite all the time spent on Mrs. Shoemaker's special dress and on Sylvie's wedding dress, Mama had managed, late in the evenings, to make another special dress . . . Jane's flower-girl dress. "After all that taffeta, and I don't like sewing on taffeta . . . makes me cringe if anyone runs a finger across it . . . well, your dress, then, was a blessing to make." Mama stroked Jane's forehead. How was it that Mama's hands were always so cool? Such a wonderful feeling, that cool hand on her forehead! Like the cool pink rose in her hands now!

Jane's dress was hanging upstairs in her little closet. Jane loved it. It was made of soft pale pink voile, about the same color as the rose she was holding. Mama had sewn a little ruffle of the same soft voile around the hem. Also, she had fashioned a wide pale pink satin sash for the waist. All was soft and pink and pretty. You opened the closet door and there it hung, completely out of the reach of Catherine-the-cat!

Catherine was a terrible problem, especially now in the summertime with screen doors that did not bang shut when you came in and went out. You had to give them a strong yank and be sure they were tightly latched, for Catherine was always lurking somewhere out of sight, and was she crafty! Leave the door ajar even a hair's breadth and she'd pry it open with her big front paw just enough for her to squeeze in; then pounce, if she could, into the middle of whatever Mama was sewing.

The Catherine problem was worse than ever now with Sylvie's filmy wedding dress occupying most of the room. So far, someone had always managed to nab Catherine midway in the air. Practically every member of the family had more than a few scratches.

Then Rufus had a good idea. That was to leave his wax-works blanket, Jane's humpy hand-crocheted rag rug, in the sleigh. Catherine had always loved that rug when it was inside the house on the brown Morris chair in the dining room, which she preferred to the green Morris chair in the parlor. She'd go to sleep under the hump; you had to be careful not to sit on her. Now she found it quite novel to discover that her private sleeping quarters had been moved outdoors. There she would pretend to sleep, but she really was listening to the birds, twitching her ears and the tip of her tail when she heard one.

Still, you couldn't count on this crafty old cat staying even in that favorite spot for long. So, "Don't let her in! Don't let her in!" remained the common warning in the Moffats' house. Even non-Moffats had been alerted to this peril. Mrs. Price would gather her skirt tightly around her ankles lest Catherine ride in on her long petticoat.

Jane laughed aloud as she thought of these funny things about their great old cat. But now here came Sylvie, the bride-to-be, walking up the path in the haphazard sort of lilting gait she had . . . like a small wave rippling sideways onto the shore.

"Hi!" she said. She stood in front of Jane and looked at her for a moment. "My little flower-girl sister!" she said. Then she took in a deep breath. "O-o-oh! Smell the roses!"

"Smell my rose," said Jane. She smiled as she watched Sylvie breathe in deeply and long its soft fragrance.

"Ah-h-h-h!" said Sylvie. "How lovely!" She tucked it in her hair.

A gentle breeze blew some petals onto Sylvie. Some of them landed in her curly brown hair, caught together in back with a narrow black velvet ribbon. "My!" she said. She laughed and shook her head. "There's a whole shower of rose petals!"

Then Sylvie went inside to try on her dress, remembering about Catherine and closing the door firmly behind her.

Until now Jane had not really taken in that there would not be many more times when she, sitting here on the porch, would see Sylvie come walking up the path in her pretty lilting way. Maybe never after tomorrow, after her wedding in the little granite church on the green. Sylvie and Ray were going to

move away from Cranbury, live in another town, in another state. The name of the town was New Rochelle. The state . . . New York.

Jane brushed away some tears. There had always been four of them; now there would be just three.

There came another gentle breeze. More of the fragrant petals floated over the fence and onto her. Suddenly Jane cheered up. "A shower of petals!" That's what Sylvie had said.

"Flower girl!" mused Jane.

So far no one had had time to tell her what she was supposed to do being the flower girl. Anyway, it was a sort of afterthought, having a flower girl. But Mama had quickly made a dress for her, and she would put that on. Then what? Of course she had the sense to know she would carry flowers. But what about her hat? Would it stay on? Mama had made her a hat, a special flower-girl hat that she might never wear again and could put in the museum . . . tack it on the wall above the Middle Bear's head.

Jane didn't like this hat. It was a flat hat with roses, not real ones, fake ones, twined around a wire brim that Mama had covered with the same pink voile as her dress.

"How can a flat hat like that stay on my head?" This worried Jane.

Once her friend, Nancy Stokes, had said, "You know what, Jane? You have a head that is a perfect oval, shaped exactly like an egg!"

"Now," Jane asked the air, "how can a flat hat stay on an egg-shaped head? Can you answer me that?"

Supposing it flew off in church and landed on somebody else's head? The minister's head, the Reverend Mr. Gandy's head perhaps. It would spoil the wedding. People trying not to laugh! Sylvie, weeping, might flee from the church, not get married, as people chased a flat hat like a hoop up one aisle and down another?

Sylvie should have chosen someone else, a cousin of theirs, any little girl with a head that was flat, to be her flower girl.

This morning, finally, she had mustered up the courage to ask Mama about a flat hat on a round head. "How will it stay on?" she had demanded.

"Don't worry," Mama had said. "You are a pretty girl, and you will be a very pretty flower girl. I'll put an elastic on your hat that will go under your chin. Then your hat will not blow off."

"Your hat will not blow off." Jane repeated these reassuring words to herself now. Even so, she was still worried.

But then, again, the soft summer breeze rustled through the

rosebushes and scattered more petals into the air. Jane had moved to the side of the porch near the fence, and now many of the pale pink petals floated down onto her hair, on her eyelashes, in her lap, and even some in her wide-open hands.

"A shower of petals!"

All of a sudden the petals gave Jane the answer as to what she, the flower girl, must do. Ah-h! The part she must play as the flower girl was to gather, as Rufus might say, circa MMMMM number of petals and strew them all the way down the aisle from the altar to the door. What a pretty sight that would be! Sylvie in her long white wedding dress lilting her way daintily down the aisle on a soft carpet of rose petals!

"Oh, my!" breathed Jane, dazzled at the thought.

She might need some help. Rufus and Joey might have to help with the strewing.

Jane looked at the petals in her hands. How soft they were! How cool! How fragrant! First, petals had flown into Sylvie's hair, then into her own, calming her fears, telling her what a flower girl must do.

The picture of a petal wedding, a rose-petal wedding, took shape in Jane's mind. Petals in the aisle, petals in the air, petals from somewhere above, fluttering down on Sylvie! She smiled, for she had a plan.

She went indoors . . . no sign of Catherine. It must be her snooze time in the sleigh under the rug with the hump. Taking no more than a quick peek into the dining room, where she could scarcely see Sylvie or Mama for the clouds of gauze and lace, she went swiftly though the little green wall-papered parlor and through the kitchen to the back entryway.

Sturdy brown bags from the grocery store were stored here. She took one of these, perfect to put rose petals in; for that is what she was going to do . . . fill many, many bags with rose petals. Out the back door she went.

She had to hurry before all the petals that were ready to fall blew away into the clouds. Naturally, she decided to begin next door at Mrs. Price's, for it had been *her* rose petals that had wafted down first on Sylvie and then on her.

Jane stood in front of Mrs. Price's house. Suddenly she felt timid. An idea inside one's head is quite different from putting it into practice. Still, why should she feel timid? Mrs. Price was a very good friend of the Moffats. So was Mr. Price. He showered them with his hose on hot days. Mrs. Price had given the Moffats many things besides Sylvie's easel. What about the little organ in the green parlor?

Bolstering herself with these thoughts, Jane walked up to the front door and rang the bell. "Take courage, Jane," she told herself. "Courage." She was so brave, you'd'a thought she was Nancy Stokes!

When Mrs. Price opened the door, Jane said, "Mrs. Price, your rosebushes are so pretty! But petals are falling off and floating away into the air. Would you mind if I picked up the fallen-off petals?"

Mrs. Price was a little deaf. It had taken a few minutes for her to answer the doorbell. It took longer for her to understand what Jane was asking.

"They, the petals, your petals, would be in Sylvie's wedding tomorrow," Jane explained.

A wide smile spread over Mrs. Price's thin and wrinkled face. She was so delighted that she rushed through the house and out the back door and met Jane at a rosebush. She shook it gently, and a shower of soft pink petals fluttered down. These, plus what were already on the ground, filled Jane's big brown bag, for they did not press the petals in. They dropped them in as gently as the summer breezes had made them fall.

"We have another rosebush on t'other fence," Mrs. Price said. "They are white ones, very delicate. I'll get another bag." This she did and shook the white rosebush gently, too. So now Jane had two big bags filled with rose petals. "Oh," said Jane. "Don't shake them all off!"

"There'll be more tomorrow," Mrs. Price said cheerfully. "They are at their height."

Mrs. Price wanted to store the bags in her cellar. "It's as cold as Greenland's icy mountains down there," she said. "They will stay fresh there."

But Jane said she and her brothers would have to get to the church very early and Mrs. Price might not be up. "Besides," said Jane, "our cellar is very cool, too. So far, Rufus's wax-works face hasn't melted. It's just a tiny bit out of shape; the mouth seems to be laughing, that's all."

Mrs. Price folded her hands. She smiled. "Yes. You are right. The petals must get to the church on time for Sylvie's wedding!" she exclaimed.

"It's because I am to be the flower girl!" Jane explained. "That's why I need lots of petals."

"Oh, I'll be there. I'm coming to the wedding all right." Mrs. Price gasped with wonderment at the whole idea. "Why, I'll see my rose petals in a wedding! Flowers before, yes! But petals, never!"

"Thank you, thank you!" said Jane as Mrs. Price went indoors, closed the strong oak door to keep the heat out, and made a note in her Line-a-Day book. "Gathered rose petals for Jane Moffat to strew at Sylvie Moffat's wedding tomorrow. Two bags full!" That made her laugh, that "two bags full."

"What a wonderful beginning!" Jane thought. She held her two precious bags lightly, not to crush the petals. She went around her house to the back door and put them on the wide and deep shelf where Rufus's waxworks mask lay on a newspaper . . . empty eye sockets staring at the dusty wooden beams above.

It was not as cold as Greenland's icy mountains down here, but it seemed cool enough to keep the petals fresh until tomorrow, the great wedding day.

Jane took some more of the sturdy brown grocery bags, and spurred on by Mrs. Price's generous donation and her delight in having her rose petals in a wedding, Jane sauntered up the street. Where next?

Practically every little house on Ashbellows Place had roses of one sort and color or another. Jane decided to ring the doorbell of every house where there were roses. She needed many, many bags of petals to have the church become all a-flutter with them.

There was only one house she decided to skip. There was a lady in that house named Mrs. Mudge, and she did not like children or many grownups. She didn't even like an old lady who came in the dandelion season, going from one lawn to the next digging out the dandelion plants with a little trowel. She

wore a wide checked apron that had a huge pouch in front . . .
a kangaroo apron . . . and she put the dandelion plants in
this.

Most people did not mind. "She probably makes dandelion
wine," said Mama. "Or maybe cooks and eats the greens."

But Mrs. Mudge did not like the dandelion lady and shooed
her away as though she were a chicken.

"My!" thought Jane as she skipped past Mrs. Mudge's house.
"Wouldn't it have been handy if I had a big kangaroo pouch of
an apron to put the petals in?" Still, the big store bags were
more sensible, especially when the time came to take them to
the church.

She rang the doorbell of the house next to Mrs. Mudge. This
lady said, "Of course, Jane. Pick up all the petals on the
ground that you want."

"I won't shake the bushes," Jane promised her as she did all
the other ladies. All were delighted to think their rose petals
would be in a wedding and be showered down onto the bride!

Some of the ladies came out themselves and gave their
bushes a little shake as Mrs. Price had done so more loose
petals would fall. "They will fall tonight anyway, in the heavy
dew," one lady said.

By now, Jane had filled all the bags she had with her and had to run home for more bags and to store the filled-up ones on Rufus's shelf.

Then back she went to the next house. "Such a sweet girl, and so bright, and to be marrying the curate, the curate of the church! And she, so young!"

Jane heard that many times. Now she crossed the street to the home of her friend, Mr. Buckle. His daughter, when she heard Jane's request, seemed reluctant. She liked Jane. Her father liked Jane and played double solitaire with her. She was not a mean lady like Mrs. Mudge.

But it came out. The reason she didn't want Jane to gather her rose petals was she saved them herself. Not for anybody's wedding, but to put them in little jars along with various spices and herbs. By Christmas she had made potpourris out of these, tied ribbons around the top, and so always had something special to give away for presents.

"Oh, dear!" said Jane. "Excuse me! I didn't know about potpourris. I won't take one single petal, I promise," and she backed down the steps. Now Jane began to worry. Supposing all the ladies on the block had really secretly wanted to save their petals and make potpourris, too? Instead, they had given them to her, not to seem stingy. She hadn't thought about potpourris for Christmas when it was June now. And she wasn't sure what a potpourri was anyway. Pots for the poor maybe?

But she felt happier when Mr. Buckle beckoned to her from his porch. She crossed the street. He handed her a little red, white, and blue striped paper bag that peppermints had come in at the drugstore. It had bright red rose petals in it.

Mr. Buckle opened it up so she could see them well. "The Buckles must be represented," he said. "There are special rose petals in here to shower on Sylvie, or she could keep them as a remembrance, for they are from a special rosebush. Miss Nellie will tell you about it."

"Oh, thank you, Mr. Buckle!" said Jane. She held the little bag in her hand, not dropping it helter-skelter into the big brown one, and just then Miss Nellie Buckle appeared at the front door. She was smiling. "I didn't like having to say no to you, Jane. But Father is right. The rose petals of the Buckles must be represented at the wedding. And another thing. I have written our name on this little bag of petals, for they have fallen from a special rosebush named after me, the Nellie B. Buckle rosebush. This bush was planted right here, in our very own garden, on the occasion of the opening of the Panama Canal, for that happened also to be my birthday. Historic petals! That's why the little bag is labeled."

Jane was stunned. "Oh, thank you, Mr. Buckle and Miss Buckle. Thank you both! My! Panama Canal petals!" And she backed down the walk, waving.

Now Jane was uneasy all over again. Labeling petals!

"Thank goodness," she thought, "nobody else told me to label their petals! When they flutter down, all will get mixed together anyway. Anyone who wants to can say, 'Did you see my Mrs. Perkins' rose petals land on the bride? On her wedding veil?' And someone else might say, 'You think so? I thought they were mine!' "

Jane decided to put the special little bag of Panama Canal rose petals under Rufus's wax face, where it wouldn't get mixed up with ordinary Ashbellows Place petals. Maybe tomorrow she would wear it inside her flat hat, tuck the little bag over her left ear, handy for whatever she wanted to do with the petals when the time came.

When she came up out of the cellar, there was Sylvie, hot and breathless . . . and excited!

"Jane!" she said. "Ray decided we should have a rehearsal for the wedding right now in church. At first we weren't going to have anyone in the wedding . . . just him and me and the minister. Then he let me have you in it. Who knows what Ray will think of next! He's sort of excited. That's why the rehearsal. I've been looking all over for you. In the apple tree, on the fences, behind the raspberry bushes! Look at your hands! Look at them! And your face! Scratches all over you! Oh, wash them! Hurry!"

Jane washed her face and hands. Mama didn't put iodine on the scratches because Jane then would have looked worse than ever. She just daubed them with peroxide. It stung a little and fizzled nicely.

Then Jane and Sylvie flew off to the church, where the Reverend Mr. Abbot was pacing, pacing, at the door.

"Ah, at last!" he said in relief. "The Reverend Mr. Gandy is here to tell us what to do and what to say when. Naturally, I, being a minister, already know. But now we have the bride here and the flower girl and myself. But let's see. If we're going to have a flower girl, we ought to have somebody to give the bride away. Not me. I'm not giving her away ever!"

He gave Sylvie a reassuring hug right there in church with the door wide open.

"But," he added, "now the wedding party is growing . . . flower girl . . . Maybe we should have a 'giver-away' of the bride. Whoever that may be should be here, too, along with us, to practice the giving away of the bride."

"Oh!" said Sylvie. "Who? Could Joey?" she said. "My brother, Joey?"

"Joey!" Ray studied the idea. "How old is Joey?"

"Fifteen now. But he will be sixteen in September. And he is taller than I am," said Sylvie.

"I'll ask the rector," Ray said.

Jane thought, "Maybe Sylvie can't get married if they don't let Joey give her away. Then, what about the rose petals so fresh and sweet and cool in the cellarway?"

But, thank goodness! Ray came back from his conference with the Reverend Mr. Gandy, who had looked in the baptism records and said that yes, Joseph Moffat had been baptized almost sixteen years ago, and a few months this side or that side of sixteen should not matter. In his opinion, Joey could be the man who would give his sister away in holy matrimony.

"So," said Ray happily, "hurry home, Jane, and tell Joey to come here as fast as he can on his bike. You can ride on the handlebars. Oh, and tell him to wear long pants. He'll look older then than he does in his knickers. We're pushing in an under-sixteen fellow to be the giver-away of the bride."

"But," said Jane, aghast for Joey, "he doesn't own any long pants!"

"Never mind for now," said Ray. "He can practice in his knickers, pull them down a little at the knees. By tomorrow, I'm sure this problem will be solved. By then he will have long pants. He could probably fit into an old pair of mine. I'm putting on weight!"

As she left the church, Jane thought, "Wait till I tell Joey about the long pants!" She grew pensive when she envisioned how Joey was going to take all of this. The man who giveth his sister away was next in importance to the bride, the groom, and almost the minister, certainly more important than her, just a little flower girl!

She'd put it to him this way. "When you think about it, Joey, isn't it nice that three of the Moffats, Sylvie, Joey, and myself, will be in the wedding?" But Rufus . . . well . . . Rufus . . . well . . . petals . . . Then an idea about the connection between Rufus and petals began to simmer in her mind.

Now, as she rounded the corner into Ashbellows Place, she spotted her two brothers coming from the other direction. She could tell they were happy. Joey was riding with one hand, holding something carefully in the other, a little polliwog, maybe. Perhaps this one will turn itself into a frog. Rufus was holding something in his tight little fist, but she couldn't guess what. He was on the handlebars.

Jane ran to meet them. "Guess what, Joey!" she said as though a wonderful surprise awaited him. "Guess what! You are going to be in Sylvie's wedding. They weren't going to have anybody in it at first. Then they added me and now you. Isn't that nice?"

No answer from Joey.

"You're going to be the man who 'giveth' his sister away!" Jane added. "How do you like that?"

A terrible cloud settled over Joey's face. He still said nothing.

Jane said pleadingly, "It has to be you, Joey, it has to be you!"

"I'm not giving my sister away," said Joey. "Once a sister, always a sister."

"It's just for the wedding that you give her away. It's part of the wedding, like a play. You have to," said Jane desperately. "They're waiting for us . . ."

"I'm not old enough," said Joey. "I'm not even sixteen. Get Sam Doody, a friend, a tall friend, who can give sisters away better than me."

"No!" said Jane. "Ray Abbot asked the Reverend Gandy. He said you can be the giver-away because you will be sixteen in September. They like a member of the family, a relative, not a friend, not even a tall friend. Only thing is you have to wear long pants."

"Well, ha-ha!" said Joey. "That really lets me out. I don't own any long pants. Go away. Ask Sam Doody. Pretend he is a distant relative. He might be for all we know . . ."

Jane felt near to crying. She visualized Sylvie, Ray Abbot, and Mr. Gandy standing at the door of the church, peering out, scanning all roads, impatient. She said, "Joey, forget Sam Doody. He has to take Mama and other people in the wedding to the church."

Rufus had listened to all this in silence. Then he said calmly, "I'll do it. I'm a brother, a real brother, not a made-up relative from ancient times. Besides"——he laughed——"I own long pants. My sailor suit pants that Mama made for the boys of the Junior Naval Reserve. I was too little to be in that, but she made me a sailor suit anyway. I can be a midget giver-away of my big sister named Sylvie Moffat."

Jane laughed. Even Joey had to laugh. But Jane said, "Well, Rufus, you really are too little. There's no way out, Joey. We have to hurry. They're there, waitin', hearts pounding . . ."

"I'll go along with you," said Rufus. "I'll help you, Joey. Do anything you say. Could be worse, you know. Could be you was the one that was getting married. Instead, you're just giving Sylvie away. It's as though it's in the syllable at school."

"Syllabus," corrected Joey.

Rufus continued as though he had not been interrupted. "And I'll stand right beside you and help you hand her over, if you want me to. Sylvie weighs ninety-eight pounds. Between the two of us we can manage."

Joey was silent. Then he said, "What about long pants?"

Jane said, "Ray Abbot says he has a pair of long pants that might fit you . . . too snug for him now," she said. "They're probably black. He always wears black."

Joey's gloom deepened. "Black!" he exclaimed.

Rufus said, "Why don't you wear your Junior Reserve Navy uniform? Nice and white and with a middy blouse that has an anchor on it. If the pants are too short, Mama will lengthen 'em. If they're too tight, she'll let 'em out."

Somewhat cheered, Joey said, "O.K."

First they went in the house and put Joey's polliwog in a basin of water. What Rufus had in his fist was a tiny turtle. "To keep the polliwog company," he said cheerfully. "When they're a little older, we'll put them back in the reservoir with their cousins and sisters and brothers, uncles, too."

Then off they rode to the church, Rufus on the handlebars, Jane on the crossbar, and Joey pedaling as fast as he could with this big passenger load. On the way, Jane said, "Rufus, maybe you shouldn't come 'cause you're not in it."

"Church is church!" said Rufus. "Church is always open. I'll go up the winding stairway to the balcony, sit in the front row, watch the proceedings, and be a stand-in (Isn't that what you call them in plays?) in case someone faints. No one will know I'm up there."

And that was what Rufus did. He slipped into church, went up the narrow stairway, and sat down in the middle of the front pew of the balcony.

Sylvie and Ray Abbot were sitting downstairs in the back pew. Their heads were craned toward the door, hoping that the rest of the wedding party would come soon. Meanwhile, they tried to pay attention to what Mr. Gandy in the pew in front was telling them about his latest trip . . . he was a great traveler. He did not seem impatient. He liked the quiet little chat he was having.

Then he interrupted himself. "Ah . . ." he said. "Here they are, the rest of the wedding party. Now, we'll commence the rehearsal."

Mrs. Peale, the organist, who had been playing hymns, practicing for both the wedding tomorrow and the Sunday service the day after, fluffed up the red velvet cushion she was sitting on and awaited the cue.

The Reverend Gandy had gone to the front of the church. He held his hand up. The cue. Mrs. Peale burst into "Here Comes the Bride!" and the wedding party proceeded solemnly to the front of the church beside the pulpit, in the formation they would repeat tomorrow.

"Too bad," Joey thought, "that this couldn't be the real thing, that they would have to do it all over again tomorrow in front of people and him with long pants of some sort or other . . ."

Jane couldn't help it. Tears rolled down her cheeks when the organist played "Here Comes the Bride." It was as though this *were* the real thing. She must be sure to bring a handkerchief tomorrow.

They went through the service very quickly. And as the organist struck up the final triumphant march and the rehearsed wedding party turned to go back down the aisle, Jane thought that this was the moment the strewing of the petals should commence tomorrow.

Right then she spotted Rufus leaning on the railing up there in the balcony in the middle of the front pew. The sun shining through the round stained glass window behind him cast a golden glow on his curly hair. Indeed, the late afternoon sun spread a lovely luminous glow over the entire church. Suddenly she envisioned clearly just how it would happen tomorrow.

All the bags of petals would be up there with Rufus, some under the pew on one side of him, some on the other. When one bag was emptied, he could reach for another. Rufus, the petal-strewer! Petals falling, falling on Sylvie, the bride, on the procession, on the ministers . . . the one doing the marrying, the other one, Ray, the one being married . . . on her, Jane, on everybody, and fall onto the aisle so Sylvie would have a soft carpet of rose petals to tread on lightly.

Wait till she told Rufus! And to Sylvie, who of course knew

nothing of this, it would be a surprise. How did she look now after the rehearsal? Had she seen Rufus?

No, Sylvie saw nothing. Her face had that radiance on it that Mama called "Sylvie's special glow."

Then Jane looked at Joey. He did not have a happy glow, and he didn't have the petal idea to cheer him up. As she and Joey were leaving the church, Rufus spinning fast as a marble around and around the spiral stairs to join them, she said, "You see, Joey? When the minister asks, 'Who giveth Sylvie away in holy matrimony?' all you have to do is to say, 'I do!' Don't say, 'Me.' Say, 'I do,' loudly so everybody hears. Now, Joey, does that sound hard? No," she answered for him. "Easy as pie!"

But Joey remained gloomy. Not that he had minded the rehearsal; it sounded very pretty. Besides, Joey always did what he had to do, go for a bushel of coal in zero weather, anything. Now, help get his sister married? All right, he'd do that. But far more than saying "I do," the thought of the long pants he didn't own bothered him. What other awful idea like wearing Ray Abbot's too tight black pants would someone come up with next?

Mama had the answer to that. When they got home, she was waiting for them on the front stoop. "Come on, Joey. While you were at the church, I went over to Mrs. Crowley's store.

There's just time to get there before she closes. You, Joey, my big son, you are going to have a brand-new suit with long trousers. I'm buying it for you. Instead of money, I told Mrs. Crowley I would alter anything her customers wanted. I'll do it all and charge her nothing until she thinks I've fixed enough . . . shortening, lengthening, whatever . . . to pay for the suit."

So Mama and Joey hurried off to Crowley's Department Store.

5

SYLVIE'S WEDDING

JANE AND RUFUS STOOD ON THE FRONT PORCH AND watched them go. Rufus seemed dejected. He said, "Joey and me always do things together. Now he's off to buy long pants." He paused. "And I'm the only one not in the wedding."

"Well, Rufus," said Jane, "you can wear *your* sailor suit, be fine for the wedding. So both Joey and you *will* be wearing long pants. *And*," she said, "you're wrong when you say you are the only one of us *not* being in the wedding. Smell! Draw in a deep breath. What do you smell?"

"Roses," said Rufus. "Roses."

"Right," said Jane. "Come on in!"

She led the way to the cellar door and opened it. My, how cool! Rufus immediately examined his waxworks face. "Hey!" he said. "What are all these big bags doing here beside my Madame Tussaud face?"

"I stored them there," said Jane. "Listen! You know what these bags are filled with? Petals of roses! I've been gathering them all day. All up and down the street. Feel in one bag. Fresh still? Don't squeeze them. Smell them! Still smell wonderful? Well, we . . . I mean *you* . . . are going to strew them on the bride. This wedding is going to be a rose-petal wedding!"

"Me!" Rufus laughed. "Me? I'm in Sylvie's wedding, too?"

"Yes. But don't tell anybody. It's a surprise. You up in the balcony strewing petals on Sylvie, the bride. Oh, I hope lots of them will land in the aisle and make a carpet of petals for her and for everybody."

"Strewing petals! I'm a good shot at miggles, but petals have never been in my field. They'll blow themselves here or there. Even a breeze might blow them out the front door."

"It doesn't matter where they fall. Look at all the bags we have! Some are bound to fall on Sylvie. Aim for her and aim for the aisle where she will walk. I'll be walking right behind her. Then will come Joey with Mama on his arm. Strew lots on

Mama if you can. Well now, isn't this a good idea? Having a rose-petal wedding for Sylvie?"

"Yeah," said Rufus. "It's O.K. The whole idea is O.K. Circa thousands, MMMMM, of petals," he murmured. "But how are we going to get all these petals to the church before twelve o'clock tomorrow? I think this wedding should be postponed. Have it in the fall. Have bright red and golden leaves shower down on Sylvie instead of rose petals."

"Can't postpone it," said Jane. "This wedding has been rehearsed, so it has to go on, come what, come may."

"I should have been in the rehearsal, scattered a few petals to get the gist of it," said Rufus.

"Oh, my goodness, no!" said Jane. "Rose petals showering down on Sylvie is going to be a surprise! Everything else is as it always is in a wedding except . . . Nancy Stokes told me this . . . that sometimes there is a page. She asked me whether or not you were going to be the page?"

"Page!" exclaimed Rufus.

"Yes. The page is usually a little boy who holds up the bride's long veil so she won't trip on it and fall down like I did that time I was a firefly. Instead of holding up Sylvie's veil, all you have to do is shower rose petals from above."

"But I'm a born page," Rufus objected. "They shouldda had me be the page!"

"I wish they had, too," said Jane. "Then all of us would be walking down the aisle. But I heard Sylvie ask Mr. Abbot, 'Ray, couldn't Rufus be my page?' He said, 'No, Sylvie, dear. We must keep this wedding simple. Flower girl? Yes. I agreed to that. But page? No.' Rufus, remember he *is* twice as old as Sylvie, so whatever he says . . . *that* has to be!"

"It's Sylvie's wedding," said Rufus. "And if Sylvie wants me to be her page," he added indignantly, "I'll be her 'simple' page. I know how to be a page, simple or not. Sylvie is used to having me be her page, not only in plays like *Cinderella*, but at home, too. At home I am her private page. So why not at her wedding?"

"Uh-hum-m," said Jane. "You're right. But who would shower the petals if you were her page?"

Rufus did not listen. "Who," he demanded, "use' to go to the library with her books so they would not be overdue and she would have to pay two cents?"

He went on. "Who use' to run to the store with her penny of the day and buy her two-for-a-penny peppermints, chocolate covered? Me! Not you, Jane. Not Joey! *Me!*"

"You, Rufus, you," agreed Jane.

"In the library, I even picked out books for her. The library lady helped me. Sylvie doesn't like the kind of books me and

Joey like . . . pirates, cowboys, and the Altsheler books. She likes histerical books."

"Historical," corrected Jane.

"And bring them back to her . . . the books and the peppermints . . . while she would be lying in the hammock looking up at the sky," said Rufus. He paused. Then he gulped. "Who's goin' to get her books and her peppermints now?"

After a pause, Jane said, "Maybe Ray Abbot will. But you, Rufus, you will be the most important person in the wedding. You up in the balcony will be a different kind of page, a petal-showerer page. Never, ever, in any story I ever read, have I heard of that special kind of page."

"Right," said Rufus. He began to laugh. "Where'd you get this idea?" he asked.

"Yesterday when Sylvie came walking up the path, a breeze fluttered some of Mrs. Price's rose petals on her. That's when I thought it up."

Rufus laughed again. "They're plenty of ordinary pages, those who hold up veils, but never before a petal-showerer in a high place casting handfuls over the railing and aiming for the bride."

They were silent for a while. Then Jane said, "You know what? I think we should take the bags of petals over to the church right now. The cellar of the church might be even cooler than ours and be like Greenland's icy mountains. Then tonight we can go to sleep in peace knowing the petals are safe and sound in the church, all ready for the showering."

Rufus thought this was a good idea. "I know just where to store them. And, Jane, they don't call the cellar of a church a cellar. They call it an undercroft. There are shelves, deep, deep shelves, right inside a narrow door to the left of the heavy big front doors. They are spooky shelves . . ."

"Just right for storing rose petals," said Jane.

Rufus got his express wagon from its garage behind the raspberry bushes. It wobbled a little, but it worked. They piled it high with the bags of petals, and off they went.

Jane ran from one side to the other to keep the bags from tumbling off. Rufus was cautious and circumnavigated the rough places in some sidewalks. It was quite a maneuver to cross a street, but they managed.

Now they were at the church. The big doors were unlocked, as always. No one was inside the church. They opened the door to the left. This narrow door led not only to the undercroft, but also to a narrow stairway, spiraling around and around upward to the balcony, and even farther up, to the ropes the sexton pulled each Sunday morning and on wedding days to make the bells peal out loud and clear.

Sam Doody often rang the bells, for the narrow, winding stairs were hard for the elderly sexton to climb.

They left the narrow door slightly ajar so that they could see something in the semidarkness. Ah! Now they could see the deep, deep shelves that seemed to be in a secret recess in the granite wall. On one side of the bottom shelf there were a few clay flowerpots. They had wilted geranium leaves and stalks in them.

"Oh, look at this!" said Jane. "There's a sign on this shelf: RESERVED FOR LADIES OF THE ALTAR GUILD."

"Means nothing," said Rufus cheerfully, "or there would be more than pots with dead geraniums in them."

"Right," said Jane happily. So they made many trips to the wagon and brought in bag after bag of rose petals. They placed them neatly on the shelf.

"Let's go," said Rufus. "But I wish I could take one bagful of these wedding petals up to the balcony and practice a little strewing . . . a rehearsal."

There was no time for Jane to say anything. At that moment they heard the heavy outer doors of the church open, and sunlight streamed in. Then came the merry sound of many ladies laughing. Jane quickly closed the narrow door. Now she and Rufus were in total darkness.

"Ts!" Jane whispered. "Maybe these are the ladies of the

Altar Guild with something for those shelves marked 're-served.' "

"I'll run up the stairs to the belfry, pull the ropes, and set the church bells pealing. That'll scare them, and they will run away!" said Rufus.

"No!" whispered Jane. "Behave yourself! This is the church." They crouched down under the wide shelf and waited tensely.

Ah-h, thank goodness! The ladies went into the church and did not even come near the little door. Jane opened it a crack. The ladies had begun to practice hymns. Even the organist had come. This must be a rehearsal for the Sunday service or . . . maybe . . . for Sylvie's wedding?

Anyway, petals, Jane, and Rufus were safe for a time. But what if another group of merry, laughing ladies arrived . . . the real ladies for whom that wide shelf was reserved?

Jane said, "Rufus, we have to change our plan. We have to put the bags of petals up under your pew in the balcony right now while they're all singing their heads off down there. Hear Mrs. Beale? We'll take the petals up to the balcony quietly, quietly, and tuck them away under the front pew. It's almost as cool inside the church as down here anyway."

"Besides, we'll have too much to do tomorrow morning, getting into our church clothes, to transport these circa MMMMM petals up to where they have to be for my showering," observed Rufus.

Jane stayed below on guard. She put bag after bag into Rufus's arms, and he sped up the spiraling stairs to the balcony and tucked them under the front pew. With one last bag in his arms and one in Jane's, they both went up to see how things looked.

Fine. The bags were tucked neatly under Rufus's pew from

one end to the other. They left one space in the middle empty for Rufus's legs and feet, which were going to have a lot to do, feeling around for the next bag to shower down "like manna from heaven," said Jane.

Jane and Rufus sat down in the empty middle space to rest for a while, and Rufus did some practicing with his legs and feet, feeling around for bag number one. "I should have a helper," he said. "No, two helpers . . . one on each side of me to shove the next bag along. How can I stretch from one end of the pew to the other, fishing for the next bag? My legs aren't long enough. Maybe I should bring a fishing rod?"

Jane laughed. "Oh, no! You'll manage. You'll be all alone up here. Nobody likes to sit in the balcony. You'll be dropping petals down below there."

"Like manna from heaven," said Rufus. "But I thought 'manna' was to eat."

"In some countries they probably do eat rose petals. Who knows?" said Jane. "But, sh-sh-sh! Different laughing ladies!"

Mrs. Beale was still practicing her solos, and other members of the choir were chiming in when they had a chance. The new laughing ladies must be . . . were! . . . the ladies of the Altar Guild, for they opened the little door to the undercroft.

Jane and Rufus crouched under the pew. "Wow!" Rufus whispered. "Rescued the petals in the nick of time!"

They listened. They heard a lady say, "Oh, Harriet, don't worry. They'll stay fresh here . . . they always have . . ."

Then they heard the little door being firmly closed, and the ladies of the Altar Guild went out of the church. The organist and the ladies of the choir left now, too. So, out of curiosity, Jane and Rufus went downstairs and looked. Moments before there had been thousands of petals on those shelves marked "reserved." Now there were many vases filled with beautiful flowers, mostly roses, this being the season for roses all over Cranbury.

"Flowers for the altar!" said Jane. "Oh, how pretty!"

"Well . . ." said Rufus. "We're lucky! We got our petals out just in time. Now all is in place for the showering tomorrow . . . if there is no more innerfering!"

They got their wagon and went home.

At home, what a sight! Wedding dress finished and kept in order on Madame-the-bust. "What an artifact!" exclaimed Rufus. Sylvie's veil was pinned up in turban-like fashion so no one would trip on it and the whole creation come tumbling down.

But more interesting than the finished wedding dress was the sight of Joey! Joey was standing on a strong oak chair, and he had on a pair of long dark brown trousers! His face was as motionless as that of a boy in a painting. He was staring at nothing except what he imagined he looked like in these long

pants. Mama was pinning up the hems of the legs, for they were too long.

When the hems were pinned up, Joey jumped down. He had on his good Sunday white shirt. He put on the vest to the suit and then the coat. After pinning these . . . a pinch here and a pinch there . . . behold Joey Moffat, a grown-up young man in a man's suit and prepared to giveth his sister away tomorrow in holy matrimony!

Rufus and Jane stood in the doorway stunned at the transformation. Mama took the mirror off the wall and balanced it against a chair. Now Joey could behold himself. Throughout all of the fitting there had been silence. Now a slow smile began to spread over Joey's face. He stood back and put his hands in his pocket. Mama put a fine linen handkerchief in his breast pocket . . . it had been Papa's. She put Joey's dollar watch in the little watch pocket. She said, "It's too bad we had to sell your father's gold watch after he died. But we did."

She tilted the mirror this way and that. Joey stood near it, a little way from it, far from it, and walked toward it to study himself from many angles.

"Gee whiz!" he said. "Is that me?"

"Joey! Joey!" cried Jane. "Joey, you look great!"

"Yeah, great!" said Rufus. But he was glad when Joey got back into his regular clothes, out of the wedding "uniform" as he called Joey's fine suit. Then Joey went out back, climbed on his blue bike, and went for a little ride.

Jane and Rufus stood and watched him disappear. "He's thinking, rehearsing in his mind," Jane explained to Rufus, "rehearsing the look of himself in his long-pants suit walking up the aisle."

"Yeh," said Rufus, "practicing being the giver-away person."

He and Jane went outdoors, edged Catherine aside, and sat

in the sleigh to get a little rest from their hard work. A few petals fluttered over the fence and into Jane's lap. She thought of all those petals under Rufus's pew. "They are really safe now, aren't they?" she asked Rufus.

He said, "Sure. All the same I know what I'm goin' to do because I don't want any innerference with the rose petals. Stay here. I'll be right back."

And he was back in just a few minutes with two cardboard signs: THIS PEW RESERVED FOR RUFUS MOFFAT. He had two thumbtacks.

"Oh, that's great!" said Jane.

So then, tired though they were, they went back to the church. There didn't seem to be anyone around now, and they thumbtacked Rufus's signs, one on each side of his pew.

"Now, that does it," said Rufus, and back home they strolled.

Joey rode up behind them. "Want a lift?" he asked.

Did they! They were so tired! Jane sat on the crossbar, Rufus on the handlebars, and they were home in no time.

Mama was now busy packing the little brown satchel that Sylvie was going to take away with her containing her "going-away" things. Mama carefully folded the pretty periwinkle blue suit she had made for Sylvie. She placed it on the top. Tomorrow, after the wedding, Sylvie would shed her bridal dress and put this blue suit on in the little room in the Parish House that was next to the kitchen. Thus she would be transformed from bride to the going-away wife of the Reverend Mr. Abbot. Mama closed the clasps of the satchel, patted it, and then went into the kitchen to prepare dinner.

"Something easy," she said. She looked tired. "Baked beans and franks, maybe?" And that it was.

They had just finished supper when, like an unexpected but welcome breeze, in rushed Sylvie with Ray Abbot following more sedately.

He said, "Good evening, Mother."

Jane and Rufus looked around to see who "Mother" was. It was Mama, of course! What a new and startling thought! "Next thing, he'll be calling me 'sister,'" thought Jane. But then they had to laugh at Sylvie. She was doing a waltz with an egg beater for a partner.

"Mama!" she panted. "Look at this!" She one-two-threed around the kitchen and into the little green parlor. "Guess what! Dottie Bridge's party was a surprise party for me . . . a shower! See what my friends gave me!"

Jane cleared the table, and Sylvie emptied her presents onto it. Three egg beaters, a can opener, a strainer, and several other useful things.

"All . . . all . . . exactly what we'll need. Isn't that right, Ray?" She gave another whirl or two around the room with egg beater number one.

Jane looked at Ray. He was loosening his clerical collar. He took the gold stud out of it, which he put into his pocket. Was he going to dance? Hurrah! Ray took egg beater number two, and he and Sylvie danced around the parlor with their egg beaters. Everybody laughed. It was fun. Mama clapped her hands and sang a New York song, "East Side, West Side," and picked up egg beater number three for a partner.

"It is the Waltz of the Egg Beaters," said Joey, gently tapping his foot and playing his harmonica.

But they left then, Sylvie and Ray, for another party. "Maybe another egg-beater party," thought Jane and went upstairs to bed. At first she couldn't go to sleep. The one-two-three of the Waltz of the Egg Beaters kept running through her head. "Could be in a fairy tale," she thought dreamily. Then she drifted off to sleep, and she did not awaken even when Sylvie slipped quietly into bed beside her.

Then it was morning.

Jane went downstairs. It was a perfect day, this last day of June, Sylvie's wedding day.

Sylvie was standing on the sturdy trying-on chair in the dining room. Mama was carefully pulling the wedding gown over her curls, which were softly tied together, neither up nor down. Then Mama arranged the veil over these loosely tied curls with a ring of pink roses, real ones, around her head. She tied the white satin sash. Sylvie put on her white satin slippers. They had little bows and looked like dancing slippers.

The slippers were the only thing not new that Sylvie had on; they were the slippers she had worn when she was Cinderella and gone in a pumpkin coach to the ball.

Then Joey helped her step down, and there stood the bride! The family gazed at Sylvie, speechless.

"Well?" she asked breathlessly. "Do I look pretty?"

"Pretty!" they all exclaimed.

"Beautiful!" said Mama, her voice shaking a little.

Sylvie looked at herself in the mirror. "Oh!" she exclaimed. "Is that me?" She kissed Mama. She said, "Oh, Mama, how happy I am!"

At ten-thirty on the dot, as had been arranged, Sam Doody drove up in his Model-T Ford. He tooted three times. Sylvie practically flew to the car like a white butterfly. Rufus had his one chance to be her page and practically flew after her holding up her filmy veil. Then off to the church drove Sam Doody with the bride!

Sam was going to come back for the rest of the family at eleven-fifteen. There was no time to be scared now. Or, if you *were* scared, you were too scared to know it. It was do this, do that, every minute.

Rufus switched from his khaki shorts into his spotless white sailor suit. He was all ready for scattering, showering, strewing thousands of petals. He stood on the railing of the porch and pretended to strew. Then he sat down in the wicker rocker and waited for Sam Doody to come up the street honking his horn.

Next Joey came out on the porch, dressed in his long-pants suit, with the spotless handkerchief in his breast pocket. He brought out a straight dining-room chair and sat stiffly in it. He examined his watch every few minutes. He looked glum. He wished he could sit up in the balcony with Rufus. He didn't even know about the petal plan.

Upstairs, Jane, with trembling fingers, took the rag curlers out of her long brown hair and brushed it a little, careful not to brush away the curls. Then she put on her pink flower-girl dress, her socks edged in pink, her white canvas slippers, and lastly her hat. She tucked the little bag with its Nellie B. Buckle red rose petals inside the crown of her hat over her left ear. The hat stayed in place nicely because of the elastic under her chin and the bag of petals.

Too bad Nancy Stokes couldn't see her now and study her head, egg-shaped no longer, flat now for the wedding. Then she went downstairs and joined the boys on the front porch. Joey got a chair for her from the dining room and waited for the honking of Sam Doody's horn. Would Mama be ready? She should be here.

Ah! Finally Mama came out. The children gasped! Was this their mama? "O-o-oh, Mama!" said Jane. "How pretty you look!"

Mama had on a white eyelet embroidered dress she had worn long ago to a ball in Madison Square Garden when she lived in New York. Because only the bride should wear white, Mama had sewn pale blue voile under the skirt and blouse so the effect was of a pale, pale blue, like an early spring sky.

"O-o-h, Mama!" Jane said again. "How pretty you look!"

"Two Cinderellas in one family," said Rufus. "And not one page between them."

Now! Now they heard it, Sam Doody's horn, honking all the way from Campbell Avenue to 12 Ashbellows Place. Pigeons and little sparrows flew away and settled on the roof of the library.

Sam's face was red and hot. Perspiration rolled from his brow half blinding him. He mopped his forehead. "Wow!" he said. "Get in! We have to hurry! Wow!"

"Why 'Wow'?" asked Rufus. He was sitting in the back seat with Jane and Joey. Joey was carrying the empty box his suit had come in. This was to put Sylvie's wedding dress in to carry home.

Mama was sitting proudly in front beside Sam. The little brown satchel with Sylvie's going-away things was on the seat between them.

"Why 'Wow'?" Rufus repeated.

"You'll see!" said Sam. "If I can get through all those . . ."

No one could hear what "all those" were, Sam was laughing so hard. Moreover his car, never a quiet one, was apt to give a sputter exactly when an important word was said. However, as they neared the green, they needed no words from Sam to tell them what "Wow" was.

People were streaming across the green from all directions. Big people, little people, old and young, even the oldest inhabitant with his cane in one hand and his left arm in Miss Nellie's right. All were dressed in their Sunday clothes.

"Wow!" said Jane. She felt her hat. Still in place with the little bag of Buckle petals to keep it steady.

"Where are all the people going?" Rufus demanded. "Is there a parade?"

"There's a parade all right," said Sam. "It looks as though

the whole town is coming. To the wedding, Rufus. To Sylvie's wedding!"

Most people were coming on foot. Even Judge Bell and his family, although they owned a big black car, were coming on foot. Many people were walking in the street. Sam had to crawl. He honked his horn almost constantly, and people parted slowly to let him through.

"Oh!" they said. "The wedding party! Where's the bride? Oh, already at the church, probably," they said.

Finally Sam reached the church and parked in front of it to let the family of the bride step down. Mama gathered her skirt carefully in her left hand and walked to the church, where she was greeted by the Reverend Mr. Gandy. Then she, Jane, and Joey went through the garden to the Parish House for Mama to cast her expert eyes on Sylvie and determine that everything was in place.

In the little room near the kitchen, there stood the nervous but happy bride surrounded by some of her friends. Mama and Jane and Joey joined her there to wait for twelve on the dot, when they would all go over to the church.

Rufus watched his family go. He stood there, feeling all alone, though dozens of people surrounded him. "Criminenty!" he said. "What am I doing here? I better get up to my pew. People are going up to the balcony. Jane was wrong when she said I'd be the only one up there, the whole place to myself for the showering!"

Rufus heard people say, "I think there are still seats upstairs in the balcony."

Then, what luck! Rufus recognized the voice of Uncle Bennie Pye, who was with his niece and nephew, Rachel and Jerry Pye. Rufus squeezed in and said to Uncle Bennie, "Would you like to sit with me? In the very front pew? That pew is reserved for me."

Uncle Bennie was delighted, so he and Rufus pushed their way through the crowd. They were little and could squeeze past the ladies in their fancy clothes making their way up the narrow stairway.

"Look!" said someone. "The front pew is empty!"

"Oh, shucks!" said another. "It's marked: RESERVED FOR RUFUS MOFFAT. And there he is!"

Rufus and Uncle Bennie had finally made it to his pew and were sitting in the middle of it. Rufus whispered to Uncle Bennie, "Feel under the pew with your feet!"

Uncle Bennie felt. "What are they?" he whispered.

"Bags of rose petals. There are bags reaching from one end to the other under this pew. I am the showerer of rose petals. You will be my assistant. We shower them on Sylvie, the bride. Jane is the flower girl. She thought this whole scheme up about the rose petals. You'll see Joey. You may not recognize him. He will have long pants on for the first time. We will scatter all these petals down on all of them when they turn around and walk out of the church. What you have to do is keep the bags moving to me. Think you can do it, keep the bags moving?"

"Oh, sure," said Uncle Bennie. "But how about the bags on the other side of you when all on this side are showered?"

"You crawl under my legs and sit on that side. Do the same thing . . . shove bag after bag to me. Maybe you can help shower them. Don't squeeze the petals. They are supposed to flutter, be soft, not get hard as peas, right?"

"O-o-h!" Uncle Bennie was delighted. "I hope mine land on my mama."

"You a good shot?" asked Rufus.

"Good at miggles. Don't know about petals yet," answered Uncle Bennie.

"Well, anyway, most of them are supposed to land on Sylvie and the wedding and in the aisle so Sylvie can tread on soft petals. Those are my orders. You and me have the main job of this wedding . . ."

"That's right," said Uncle Bennie happily.

Rufus turned around. The balcony was filled up. People were standing all along the walls by the steps leading down to where he was sitting. He felt selfish sitting here with just Uncle

Bennie. He spotted Hughie Pudge, a boy he had known since Room One, Wood Street School. He beckoned to Hughie. Hughie came down and sat on the other side of Rufus, so Uncle Bennie would not have to do all the shoving of bags to Rufus. Hughie got the gist just as fast as Uncle Bennie had and felt for his first bag after practically standing on his head to get a look at them.

"Wowie!" was all he said.

Rufus saw Rachel and Jerry Pye looking longingly down at their little uncle. Rufus beckoned to them. He wagged his head up and down. "Sure, come on down," that shake of his head meant, and they came down and sat beside Uncle Bennie. Uncle Bennie passed the word to them as to why this pew had been reserved for Rufus.

There were still a few empty seats. Rufus whispered to a nice lady behind him that she could pass the word back that a few more children, not grownups, could pile in here. That the lady did, and just in the nick of time the three little daughters of Judge Bell squeezed their way into Rufus's pew. The organist had begun playing melodies, not the bridal music yet, but music to put the congregation in a quiet and expectant mood. Now the pew was full, and Rufus was not lonesome any more.

The word was passed all along in a soft whisper to the newcomers about the big bags of petals under the pew. The littlest

Bell girl . . . her nickname was Noonie . . . in leaning over to see them, lost her hat, and it floated down over the balcony to who knew where? Her sisters were ashamed of her.

Of course Rufus and Company could not see underneath the balcony, but from the way the congregation was acting, they knew the members of the wedding party must be gathering in the doorway.

Sam Doody, after taking a swift glance inside the balcony, went up the rest of the spiraling stairway to the belfry tower, and he pulled the ropes that made the wedding bells peal out. So, joyously, the bells pealed forth announcing to the rest of the people of Cranbury that Sylvie Moffat's wedding was about to begin.

Their echo had hardly died down when the organist struck up the wedding march. Everybody stood up and turned to watch Sylvie's entrance. Uncle Bennie was so excited that he almost reached now for a bag of petals to throw, forgetting that it was *after*, not *before*, the ceremony that he was to help strew.

But Rufus stopped him in time. He spotted Mama and his aunt, Tonty, and many others he knew . . . Mr. Buckle and Miss Nellie . . . some of the teachers. Then, leaning over the railing, the children in the front row saw the wedding procession. First, there was Jane, the flower girl, clutching her hat with one hand and holding a big bouquet of pink roses in the other. And next, on the arm of her brother Joey, was Sylvie, the bride, looking like a fairy-tale princess, walking in that lilting way she had. She did not trip even though she had no page to hold her long veil, which spread out behind her like feathers of a white fan.

The minister was standing at the head of the aisle waiting for all the members of the wedding to converge here. Ray Abbot came from the side door that led to the Parish House and waited for Sylvie and Joey to reach the minister.

When the members of the wedding were all in place, the Reverend Mr. Gandy began the service. He had a nice smile on his face. "Probably could see that Joey was scared," thought Rufus. "Maybe Sylvie and Jane were, too."

Rufus whispered to Uncle Bennie, "See that man there in long pants? That's my brother, Joey. Hard to believe, but true."

Rufus barely heard the words of the ceremony, just the "Do you takes?" and the "I dos." But he heard Joey answer "I do!" in a clear, strong voice that even people in the back of the balcony could hear when he was asked the giveth-away question.

It was time for Ray to put the ring on Sylvie's hand. He fumbled for it in his vest pocket, where he rarely put anything, placed it on her finger, and said, "With this ring, I thee wed . . ." Ray Abbot kissed the bride, and Jane, who had been holding Sylvie's bouquet during the ceremony, gave it back to her. Those in the wedding then turned around, and the triumphant march began.

Now! Now was the time for the showering of the petals, for slowly Sylvie, on Ray's arm, began to walk down the aisle.

"Criminenty!" said Rufus. "It's now or never!" He reached down under his pew, and as the bride and groom slowly, slowly, came down the aisle smiling, blowing kisses, Rufus sent the first large handful of rose petals fluttering down.

It was the signal. All the children to the right and to the left of Rufus reached under the pew for a bag and began to shower their petals down. You would think they had had a rehearsal! They didn't let all of them shower down at once. They let them fall, one handful at a time, so the church was filled with thousands of petals gently floating all around.

"It's lucky I have lots of helpers," thought Rufus. "I could never have handled all this business by myself." Why was he crying? He whisked away a tear, and Uncle Bennie handed him the next bag.

More tears to whisk away. There was Sylvie halfway down the aisle treading lightly on the soft petals. But she paused. She looked up at the balcony, saw Rufus up there in the middle, and blew him a kiss. Was she smiling or crying? He let a whole bagful of petals fall down on where she stood, and she seemed to catch some in her upstretched arms. Many landed on her

veil, and hundreds fluttered all up and down the aisle where she was walking.

So it really was as Jane had dreamed. Being a flower girl really had meant having petals from all the rosebushes on Ashbellows Place fall onto Sylvie, the bride, her sister. A rose-petal wedding!

The last member of the wedding was the Reverend Mr. Gandy, who seemed astonished but pleased. He looked up at the balcony, and he saw Rufus, and Rufus showered the last of the petals down on him. Many fell into the wide sleeves of his surplice as he raised his arms in a kind of a salute to the children up there.

Now Rufus and his friends could no longer see the wedding procession. And now the people in the balcony were in as much of a hurry to get downstairs to greet the bride as they had been to find a place to sit before the ceremony began. They wanted to kiss the bride and wish her happiness forevermore.

Sam Doody made his way through the throng and up to the belfry again to make the church bells ring out. So the bells pealed out and perhaps could be heard as far away as Savin Rock since it was such a clear day.

People had rushed down from the balcony and disappeared. Uncle Bennie, Rachel and Jerry, and the three little Bell girls all had left. Rufus was sitting alone with bags and bags, empty rose-petal bags. What was he supposed to do next?

Ah! Rufus was not forgotten. Jane rushed up to the balcony. "Oh, Rufus! Rufus! You were wonderful!" she said. "You and all your friends . . . wonderful! Now, guess what! We are all to go to the Parish House and have good things to eat and have a piece of the wedding cake. Everybody is invited."

Rufus revived. He had been thinking he should have brought a peanut-butter sandwich along with the petals yesterday and put it under his pew.

So he and Jane went to the Parish House. Sylvie spotted Rufus and hugged him. "No one ever had such a pretty wedding before. All those petals . . . see?" She shook her head, and some fell out of her curls.

Rufus smiled. "There were circa MMMMM or more of them," he said.

Sylvie, half laughing, half crying, was radiant. Little folding chairs that were used for plays or Sunday School had been brought out and lined the room. In the middle was a long table with a huge wedding cake on it and wonderful things to eat: salads, sandwiches, pink lemonade . . .

Then Sylvie made the first cut into the cake. Some wrapped their piece in a paper napkin to take home, put under their pillow, and make a wish. Some ate their piece right away. Some said they were going to wrap theirs in wax paper and put it in their memory book along with as many rose petals as they could scoop up.

Then Sylvie went up on the little stage where she had performed often in Sunday School plays. She stood still, looking the guests over.

"Ah-h-h!" said Mrs. Price. "She is going to throw her bouquet!"

All the young girls crowded to the front, hoping to be the one to catch it and then, surely, to be the next bride in the town of Cranbury.

Sylvie paused a moment, looking at her eager friends with their outstretched arms. But she had someone in mind. It was Dottie Bridge, her best friend, she was aiming for, and she aimed correctly. Dottie caught the bouquet and hugged it to her. Ray Abbot lifted Sylvie off the stage, where, he said, long ago he had seen little Sylvie in *Cinderella* and loved her forevermore right from then.

While people stood around and talked and ate some of the good things, Sylvie disappeared into the little room by the kitchen and changed her clothes. She put on her periwinkle blue suit. Mama was in there helping her, and she put the wedding dress in Joey's long-pants suit box. Mama kissed

Sylvie good-by and she kissed Ray, and Sylvie and Ray slipped away.

Mama joined Rufus and Jane and Joey, and they went outside. Someone had written JUST MARRIED in white chalk on Sam Doody's car. Others had tied pink-and-white crepe-paper streamers to the back. Sylvie and Ray stepped into the back seat. Ray had Sylvie's little brown satchel, and he put that on the front seat with Sam.

Mama and Jane and Joey and Rufus stood beside the car. People rushed out of the Parish House to say good-by and to wave! Just in time, Jane remembered the little candy bag filled with the Nellie B. Buckle red rose petals. She handed them to Sylvie, said they were special petals from a rosebush in the oldest inhabitant's garden. Sylvie tucked them in the brim of her hat. "Thank him! Tell him I'll save them always!" she cried, for now she was really crying a little.

"Write to me! Write to me! The petals were so lovely . . . beautiful . . . thank you all!" She blew a kiss to Joey, who was standing a little apart. "My big little giver-away-of-the-bride brother! Good-by!" she called out to him loudly, for Sam Doody was cranking up the car now. With a shudder the engine caught on, and slowly the car started up.

Then many of the ladies of Ashbellows Place who had brought little bags of petals for this very moment threw them at the bride and groom. So off they went in a shower of petals caught in the breeze and seeming to scamper after the car as it went slowly down the street.

"Much nicer than throwing rice," said Judge Bell. "I always thought, my, what a terrible waste! Throwing away good rice with so many people starving in the world . . . everywhere . . ."

Sam drove slowly so people could follow them down Church Street to the corner, crying, "Good-by! Good-by! Happiness always . . ."

Then Sam turned to the left onto Campbell Avenue, and with much tooting and honking he drove down the avenue on the way to the Cranbury depot to catch the three-fifteen train to New York City.

People began to drift away. Some children were scooping up the new shower of petals. "To make a bed for my dolly . . ." said Noonie Bell. Her hat had been found. It had fallen on the baptismal font, but not in it.

More and more people, after shaking hands with Mama and Joey, telling Jane how pretty she looked, left. Soon all had left.

Now, just Mama and Rufus and Joey and Jane were standing alone at the curb. Joey went into the Parish House to get Sylvie's wedding dress and quickly came back to stand with his family. They were straining their necks for one last glimpse of

Sylvie that they might get when Sam drove past the White Church on the green.

They did see her! Sam Doody honked his horn loudly to show that Sylvie and Ray had seen Mama and all of them, too. Then he stepped on the gas, and now they were out of sight.

The Moffats stayed for a few minutes longer, slowly letting their waving arms drop to their sides. Then quietly they walked across the green and went home. They were trying to get used to the idea that Sylvie had really left home. No one said a word.

In the house, Jane took her flower-girl hat off right away. But she kept her pink dress on. Mama took her hat off, too. But she kept her pretty dress on, too. There were still petals in her hair and in Jane's.

The boys had disappeared upstairs as fast as possible to change into their khaki shorts. Maybe Mr. Price would get the hose out later and cool them off?

Mama and Jane didn't know what to do. They just sat. And the wedding seemed like a dream.

6

CONVERSATION OVER THE BACK FENCE

THE WONDERFUL LONG DAYS OF SUMMER WERE SLIPPING by with swimming, hiking up the Sleeping Giant, picnics up on Peter's Rock in Montowese or at Lighthouse Point, just walking around town looking for things for the Moffat Museum, or just plain seeing the sights: fireworks on the green or over the Long Island Sound in Savin Rock. There were so many things to do in Savin Rock, especially to hear the famous band of John Philip Sousa on some Sunday afternoons. Sometimes even Mama went to hear Sousa, too.

But now Jane was going to see some sights somewhere else. A little while ago Mama had said, "Jane, how would you like to take a little trip? Go down to New Rochelle and visit Sylvie and Ray, see the pretty little house they live in, and the little wooden church where Ray is the minister. See all the sights around their town: the woods, the brooks, the river, the amusement park at Rye Beach, not far away from them."

"O-o-oh!" cried Jane. "And how would I get there?"

"On the train," said Mama. "All by yourself. Tomorrow."

"Me? On the train? All by myself?" asked Jane. "Tomorrow?"

"Uh-hm-m," said Mama. "All by yourself and stay for a whole week. Sylvie is lonesome and wants to see her little sister."

"Just me?" repeated Jane.

"Uh-hm-m," said Mama. "Just you this time. Another time the boys will go, when Joey is not so busy as he is now. It's nice at Sylvie's. You'll like it. You know how much I loved my visit there."

"And I cooked the dinner here that night," said Jane.

"Yes," said Mama. "Sylvie and Ray now have a car, exactly like Sam Doody's. They call it 'Wheezy.' Takes it quite a while to get going, lots of cranking ups, but then it catches its breath and away you go for a little joy ride!"

"Oh, my!" said Jane.

Mama said, "They might meet you at the station in Wheezy. But if not, you take a trolley marked 'South Third Street,' even though it will be going north. Coming back to the station, it *will* be coming south. See?"

"Confusing!" said Jane.

She went outdoors in a daze and climbed up on Mrs. Price's fence to think this trip over, to get it straight in her mind. Tomorrow! Sylvie had sent the money for her train tickets. It had just come. Mama showed it to her. It was true.

Jane was excited. She wished Nancy were home so she could tell her, discuss this amazing event with her. But Nancy was still away in Maine. If she were here, she would rehearse with Jane all steps of the journey. Nancy had once gone all by herself to Camp Minnetonka . . . train, horse-and-wagon, what-all . . ."

Anyway, Mrs. Price's high fence was a good place for her to rehearse by herself all stages of the coming journey. "First," she told herself. Ah, but then, what luck! At that moment Mrs. Price came out of her back door with a large wicker basket filled with wet clothes. Maybe she would be interested and would discuss a trip like this with Jane?

Tomorrow! Jane thought that when you went on a trip, you ought to pack at least one whole week in advance. She'd talk this over with Mrs. Price. Mrs. Price had told her how to cook the dinner that time when Mama went away for the day. She was always helping. The trip could be like a lesson in geography. You get on a train that goes west. You get off at New Rochelle. You get on a trolley marked South Third Street, but it will be going north. Coming back to the station, vice versa, still marked South Third Street, but really coming south now, coming back to the New Rochelle railroad station.

Jane wondered if Mrs. Price was good in geography. As for her, Jane, she got an "A" on her report card every month in geography. She could still remember, even though it was vacation time, where the Housatonic River rose and where it ended up. In Long Island Sound!

She studied Mrs. Price, who plumped her basket of wet clothes on the grass and made ready to hang them up. She wore an apron, blue checked like Mama's, but her apron had a big pocket in front to hold the clothespins. So Mrs. Price's apron was really more like the dandelion lady's apron. Mrs. Price, for the fun of it, if she wanted to, could go up and down Ashbellows Place and dig up dandelion plants and pretend she was the dandelion lady herself grown skinny.

Mrs. Price didn't do that. She put one of her clothespins in her mouth, ready for when she needed it. It might be thought of as the beginner, that clothespin, a captain clothespin.

Mrs. Price did not notice Jane sitting up there on the fence watching her. She must have thought she was alone in the whole world, for when she didn't have a clothespin in her mouth, she said something out loud, nodded her head, and answered it whatever it was. She seemed to agree with everything she was saying. There were no frowns or angry shakes of her head. She was in a good mood, enjoying herself.

"But," thought Jane. "Maybe she is lonesome, talking to herself that way, laughing, nodding her head as though she has an imaginary companion and they are sharing a joke or some new piece of news. Maybe she'd like a real live companion, like me. Maybe she would like to hear about the plan of my trip tomorrow, first train, then trolley, then walk. Maybe she would like to pretend that she is the teacher and I am a member of her class in geography. Or maybe it should be vice versa, me be the teacher, she a member of the class. We'll see how it goes. I'll start from the beginning," thought Jane, "and talk fast before she reaches the far end of the clothesline."

Jane said, "Hello, Mrs. Price!"

It was lucky it wasn't vice versa here, for had Mrs. Price

been the one sitting on the fence, she might have fallen off. She was that much taken by surprise to hear a human voice when all along she had thought no one else was around.

"You sittin' on the fence there, Jane, and I never knew it," she said. She gave a friendly nod, put her clothespin back in her mouth, and smiled on one side of her mouth. It had to be a crooked smile with that clothespin there.

"I'm going on a trip tomorrow," said Jane. "A train trip!"

Mrs. Price nodded her head up and down and raised her eyebrows, indicating she had absorbed that piece of information and what next?

"All by myself," said Jane.

Mrs. Price opened her eyes wide and looked Jane straight in the face. She raised her eyebrows again, and this seemed to ask the question, "Where?"

"I'll tell you," said Jane. "But, Mrs. Price, would you like to pretend you are my teacher and that you call on me in geography class and you ask me this question, 'How do you get from Cranbury, Connecticut, 12 Ashbellows Place to be exact, to a little town in New York named New Rochelle, 509 South Third Street to be exact.' And then I would tell you and maybe you would give me an 'A' for giving the right answer?"

Mrs. Price nodded.

Jane persisted. "This could be like a rehearsal, you know."

Mrs. Price nodded again. "Let the rehearsal begin!" she said. This time her captain clothespin fell out of her mouth, but landed neatly in the pouch pocket of her apron. She fished it out. "She likes that one," thought Jane, and Mrs. Price chewed on it the way a man chews on a cigar.

"All right," said Jane. "Now, I'll begin the rehearsal, the story from the beginning, the way it is supposed to happen anyway. All the steps of the journey."

"First," prompted Mrs. Price.

"First," said Jane, "Joey is going to ride me on the crossbar of his bike from 12 Ashbellows Place to the Cranbury depot."

"Don't need to know much geography to know where that depot is," said Mrs. Price with a laugh. "You get an 'A' so far."

Jane laughed, too. "No," she said. "Well, once there, I am to catch the eight-fifteen train to New York. The eight-fifteen is not the Bankers' Express. That important train does not stop in Cranbury."

"Cranbury is important," objected Mrs. Price.

"Yes, but not to bankers," said Jane. "But, remember this, Mrs. Price. I am not a banker going to New York. I am a girl going to New Rochelle!"

"Sounds like a cheese!" observed Mrs. Price.

"Yes," agreed Jane. "Sounds like a cheese. But I must take

the eight-fifteen and not make a mistake and take a train that doesn't stop there, because Sylvie and Ray Abbot live there now, and I don't want to be on a train that goes whizzing by their New Rochelle depot and land in New York with the bankers."

"Right!" said Mrs. Price.

"*My* train, the eight-fifteen, stops everywhere all along the way from here to New York City, every possible place between here and New Rochelle."

"I keep thinking it's Neufchâtel like the cheese," said Mrs. Price.

"I'll tell Sylvie that when I get there," said Jane, laughing. "But in this rehearsal, and way before the cheese station, well, me and Joey haven't even gotten to the Cranbury Station yet. When we do, the eight-fifteen will come along and, being a local, it will stop! A gush of steam will rush up from underneath. That always scares me, and that is one reason we're having this rehearsal right now, to practice not being scared."

"Want me to make a sound like a gush of steam coming up from under a train?" asked Mrs. Price.

"No, thank you," said Jane. "I'm practicing not being scared. I know what the steam sounds like, thank you all the same. Oh, you should have reminded me . . . the ticket? Do I have a ticket? No. Joey and me will buy the ticket while we wait for the eight-fifteen, round-trip ticket, going to Neufchâtel and coming home."

"New Rochelle!" said Mrs. Price. "I'll have to give you A minus if you don't get it straight in this geography lesson."

"Well, while the steam is gushing forth, with my ticket in my hand, I must get up those high steps. They must make the steps of trains for six-feet-high people like Judge Bell and Sam Doody, not little boys and girls. But Joey will give me a boost, a shove, and he will push my satchel in after me . . . my nightgown and things, my pink dress. The train stops for only about a minute. I have a new nightgown."

Mrs. Price nodded. "That's nice," she said. "A nightgown!"

"You didn't think I was coming back the same day, did you? Well, I'm not. I am staying one solid week!"

Mrs. Price nodded. "A long stay. I'll miss you."

"What a listener!" marveled Jane. But who wouldn't listen to such a story, a story that hadn't even happened yet! "Well, so now I am on the train and I stay on the train until I get to . . ."

"New Rochelle!" interrupted Mrs. Price, who was proud of her fine memory.

"Yes!" said Jane triumphantly. "But there, there will be many trolleys at the station to choose from, and I must find the one that says 'South Third Street.' Mama says it will be going north, but it will be marked 'South.' Coming home, back to the station, the sign makes more sense because we *will* be coming south."

"Lazy," observed Mrs. Price. "Can't even change the south to north."

"Perhaps the trolley people in New Rochelle are not as smart as the trolley people in Cranbury, where they change Savin Rock to Lighthouse Point or vice versa. Mrs. Price, have you ever heard of South Third Street in New Rochelle?" Jane had to speak a little louder now because Mrs. Price and her basket of wet clothes were moving farther and farther down the clothesline.

Mrs. Price heard though. She shook her head ruefully. "And I'm supposed to be the teacher . . . the geography teacher . . ."

"Don't mind," Jane pleaded. "Probably nobody else I know ever heard of it either. And maybe the people in New Rochelle never heard of Ashbellows Place in Cranbury. 'Vice versa,' as Rufus would say. Has that struck you?"

"Well, the way you put it, it struck me now," said Mrs. Price.

"Well, me neither, until Sylvie moved there. Then, coming home, one week from tomorrow, I do the whole thing backwards."

"Just like that trolley car that goes south or goes north," said Mrs. Price.

"Well . . . sorta," said Jane.

"I think you're smart. If I am your pretend teacher, I give you an 'A.' Forget the minuses. Any little girl that can go to a foreign town and take a trolley marked south when it means north deserves A+. Have a nice time! Maybe you will send me a post card?"

"O-o-o-h my, yes!" said Jane. "Maybe I'll send you two." She thought a moment. "I'll send post cards to everybody on Ashbellows Place besides my brothers and Mama."

"A week of writing post cards, sounds like," said Mrs. Price.

"I write fast," said Jane.

"You'll see wonders," said Mrs. Price. She had finished hanging up her clothes now. She picked up the empty wicker basket. She was going to go indoors.

Jane, who had slid along the fence, even picking her way through the rosebushes carefully so she would not get scratched, didn't want to lose Mrs. Price, have her go in. She slid her way rapidly back to the end near Mrs. Price's back door. Mrs. Price already had one foot up on the bottom step and was now reaching for the handle of the screen door.

"Wait! Please wait, Mrs. Price. There is one thing that bothers me . . ."

"Worse than the gush of steam?" asked Mrs. Price.

"Well, different," said Jane. "I don't know what to do about packing, when to do it. What would you do? This has nothing to do with geography any more. It's just an ordinary question. If . . . if you was me, what would you do? Would you pack tonight and then go to bed, and everything, your satchel and your pocketbook, would be ready when you got up? Or would you go to bed early, get a good night's sleep, get up early when you hear a rooster crow, cock-a-doodle-do, and then pack?"

Mrs. Price put her wicker basket down on the top step. "So she can think better," Jane imagined.

Mrs. Price then said, "Well, I've thought it over, Jane. What I think the wise thing to do, if it was me, not you, traipsin' all down the track, is to get all my packing done tonight and not listen for the rooster. Not taking a big trunk anyway, are you? Like I have in my attic?"

"No," said Jane. "It's a little straw satchel."

"No matter what. Trunk . . . little straw satchel . . . paper bag, I know if it was me, I would pack tonight. Then, in the morning, nothing to it but eat your breakfast, tie your satchel on the back of Joey's bike, put yourself on the crossbar, sideways . . . tuck in your skirt so it don't get caught in the spokes . . . and you and Joe go, just plain go, to the Cranbury depot.

Step one in the geography lesson. How's that?"

"Yes," said Jane. "I think you are right. That's what I tended to think would be right, too. Well, two heads are better than one, right, Mrs. Price?"

"Depends on the heads," declared Mrs. Price. "And don't worry about your museum. I'll keep an eye on it if the boys aren't around. I might, just for fun, get into the sleigh before Mr. Price gets home. Then he'll say, 'Aggie! What the dickens!' seeing me over there in the sleigh. You can be sure, Jane, nobody is going to come in and steal some artifact . . . my old easel or anything . . . while you are away!"

"Good!" said Jane. "But, remember, it is free . . ."

"Right," said Mrs. Price. "But," she added ruefully, "I thought it would have been nice to sit up there with a little tin cup . . . not charge to go into the museum, but just collect a penny or two for the starving people of Armenia, or anywhere . . ."

"Well, maybe you should do that down at the green, not in our museum sleigh. More people down there. Anyway Joey or Rufus will be around most of the time. So, so-long, Mrs. Price. I may not see you again before I go."

Mrs. Price picked up her basket and waved to Jane as though Jane were already on her train pulling out of the depot.

Jane went indoors, too. For a while she stood in her room, and she didn't know quite what to do between now and evening . . . packing time. Why wait for evening? Why not now? She had never packed a satchel with enough clothes to last one whole week, just a small amount of things for a day at the beach or up on Peter's Rock.

So she spread out on her bed everything she was going to take. She laid them beside the satchel. Then she put on a chair the clothes she was going to wear. She whitened her canvas slippers, including the narrow strap across the instep. And she washed and dried her comb. Now all was ready for filling the satchel.

She went back outdoors. She tidied up the museum. She jumped rope, played hopscotch, went to the corner to watch the trolley cars and raced one to the library at the next corner and won. What next?

Would the day ever come to an end? Finally it did. Dinner was over. Mama lighted the little gas jet on the wall so Jane could see what she was doing. Mama said she would put it out when Jane had finished.

So now to pack! Jane packed her satchel and unpacked it and packed it again. Sometimes she put her pink dress on top, sometimes her nightgown. She finally left it with her nightgown on top. She fastened the two clasps. They didn't seem very strong. She got a cord from the kitchen and tied it around the satchel, so neither her nightgown nor her pink dress would go flying out the train window.

She put her little red patent leather pocketbook on the chair beside the blue dress she would wear. It had some nickels, some dimes, and a one-dollar bill in it, also a little envelope that had the exact amount of money to buy her ticket to and from the town of New Rochelle. She had a handkerchief in her pocketbook with her name  embroidered in the corner, a birthday present from her aunt Tonty. If she saw a sad sight, or a funny one, both of which could make her tears flow, she could wipe her eyes.

Then she went to bed. Mama came up, turned off the gaslight, and put the littlest oil lamp on a bureau in the hall, where it always stayed on during the night in case anyone was afraid of the dark. Jane used to be, but not any more.

She thought about the day. She thought about her conversation over the back fence with Mrs. Price . . . the rehearsal for the big day tomorrow, as they had gone over it. Finally she went to sleep while still rehearsing and going over in her mind the stops on the train between Cranbury and Neufchâtel . . . no . . . New Rochelle . . .

Would the real trip tomorrow be as had been rehearsed?

7

JANE ON THE EIGHT-FIFTEEN

IN THE BEGINNING, JANE'S TRIP ON THE EIGHT-FIFTEEN
went exactly as she and Mrs. Price had practiced it yesterday in
their conversation over the back fence. She woke up when the
sun rose and the rooster crowed.

There was bound to be a surprise or two, especially for
someone like Jane who had never before gone on a train all by
herself. She felt excited and happy. No wonder people liked to
travel, going somewhere, anywhere, to a near or faraway

place. She dressed quickly, put on her blue dotted-Swiss dress, her shoes and her socks, and sat down on the front porch. She had her satchel beside her. On top of it, she put her little red patent-leather pocketbook and her white pique hat, with its make-believe red cherries around it.

She seemed to be the only person up anywhere. Dew sparkled on the grass. The trees and bushes looked brighter and fresher than usual. How sweet was the smell of honeysuckle on the fences, how pungent the smell of the hop vines growing by the porch! She rocked back and forth, back and forth, in the green wicker rocker, waiting for the sound of someone indoors waking up.

At last, there were sounds of stirring and the smell of Mama's coffee brewing on the stove! Then time spun as rapidly as the needle of a compass if you turned it this way and that. She went in, had some Post Toasties, and now the trip was about to commence!

Joey tied her satchel to the back carrier behind the seat of his bike; Jane kissed Mama good-by, got on the crossbar, and with a wave to the whole of Ashbellows Place, she and Joey were off. She was on her way to the Cranbury depot, the first leg of the journey, to get herself on the eight-fifteen.

Joey was riding lickety split because he wanted to be under the bridge when the Bankers' Express roared by above it. Jane didn't like noise and, thank goodness, the express streaked by just before Joey reached the bridge. So now Jane and Joey rode under the quiet bridge and up the pebbly slope to the depot.

The depot was a small brown clapboard building. Jane thought it looked like a cute little house to live in. That's what the pigeons thought, too. There was a cupola on top, and now the pigeons settled themselves on it, recovering from the unsettling occurrence of having the Bankers' Express go whizzing by. Beady-eyed, they surveyed the tracks for a crumb or two.

Jane hopped off the bike. Joey unstrapped her satchel, and they went in to buy her ticket. The station had a musty smell of stale tobacco and other stale smells from years long gone by.

A man in a shiny dark blue coat was standing behind the window. "Ticket? Where to?"

Breathlessly Jane said, "I'd like a round-trip ticket to New Rochelle. Have you ever heard of it?"

"Sure," said the man. He reached behind him, and from a shelf with lots of little cubicles in it, he pulled out the ticket he wanted.

It came in two parts, one saying "Cranbury to New Rochelle," the other saying "New Rochelle to Cranbury." Jane paid him and put the ticket in her red patent-leather pocketbook.

"I'm going on the eight-fifteen," said Jane. "Is this the right ticket for that special train?"

"Sure," said the man. "Or for any local train. The eight-fifteen from New Haven to Grand Central Station will be along in a few minutes."

"It will stop in New Rochelle, won't it?" asked Jane anxiously.

"Has to," said the man. "It's a local . . . stops at every hen coop all down the line." He laughed. "Every hen coop," he repeated.

Jane went outdoors and stood beside Joey, who had put her satchel at the place on the platform where he figured the door of a coach would stop.

"Listen, Jane," said Joey. "Remember what Mama always says. Don't speak to strangers."

"Supposing a stranger speaks to me?" asked Jane.

"Look straight ahead. Eye them out of the corner of your eyes. Even if, out of the corner of your eyes, that person appears to be nice, sounds nice, look straight ahead. Say nothing. That's the way to deal with strangers."

Now, way down the tracks where they seemed to merge together, they saw a train coming closer and closer.

"The eight-fifteen," said Joey. He looked at his watch. "On time," he said.

The stationmaster came out and stood beside a cart with canvas sacks of mail on it.

"This *is* the eight-fifteen to New Rochelle, isn't it?" asked Jane. Her heart was beating hard.

"Yes, miss. It's that," he said. "On time."

The train came to a sudden screeching stop. Pigeons flew up into the sky. Jane rushed to the door of the nearest coach. There was no time to be concerned about the gush of steam hissing from underneath that enveloped her. Joey boosted her up the high steps while the conductor grabbed her from above. Joey picked up her satchel and shoved it up onto the train. She and her satchel and a huge fat timetable that Joey had given her as a surprise present were all together on the eight-fifteen train.

The stationmaster had flung the sacks of mail into a car up ahead. Then the conductor blew a whistle. " 'Board! 'Board!" he said.

Jane sat down by a window near the back of the car, tucked her satchel under her seat so no thief would get it, looked out the window, saw Joey, waving, waving, and waved back. He had his foot on the pedal, ready to go the minute the train went. She knew he was going to ride his bike beside the train to the end of the platform, wave as long as possible, and then good-by to Jane on the eight-fifteen!

The train started up! Puff-puff-puff, puff-puff, going faster and faster, and Joey was out of sight. But she was off, off on her first train trip all by herself!

So far, all was going along exactly as practiced yesterday with Mrs. Price. "Probably putting out more laundry," thought Jane fondly, while she, Jane Moffat, was speeding down the tracks on the eight-fifteen.

The seats on this train were a dusty red plush, faded and smelling of train. Jane settled herself comfortably and looked around. That must have been the reservoir they had just sped past. The conductor sat down across the aisle, behind the last seat on that side. He had a little red plush seat to sit on that folded itself up and sprang back whenever he stood up. He stood up now.

"Tickets!" he said. "Tickets!"

Jane got out her ticket, and since she was in the rear, he came to her seat first. He tore off the "to New Rochelle" half, punched it, and stuck it in a little slit in the back of the seat in front of Jane. She could keep an eye on it there. That ticket proved she was on the right train and not on one taking a surprise turn up an unusual switch leading to a destination unknown.

Jane put the other half of her ticket, the "to Cranbury" half, back in her pocketbook for the time when the final stage of this expedition would take place.

The conductor pivoted around on his big flat black shoes as though he were on a turnstile and held out his hand for the ticket of a lady in the seat opposite Jane's. He examined her ticket closely. Jane watched. The lady was elderly.

"Oh, yes!" said the conductor. "You're the lady from Montowese bound for Greens Farms. I've been told to watch out for you and see that you get off there." He punched her ticket and put it in the slit in the back of the seat in front of her. "You're Ida Brooks, right?"

"No!" said the lady indignantly, "I'm *Ada* Brooks. On my way to visit Cousin Agnes."

"Ida . . . Ada . . . what's the difference so long as you're one or the other. *Brooks* is what counts. I'll see that you get off at Greens Farms. Don't you worry, don't you worry one bit," said the conductor.

Then he got out a shiny black leather notebook and put a check in it. "Probably," thought Jane, "besides the lady from Montowese, he has other people on this train he has to keep track of. Well, he doesn't have to keep track of me. I know where I'm going. New Rochelle!"

The conductor moved on up the aisle. He had put his notebook back in his pocket. When he reached the front door of the coach, he proclaimed loudly in train language, the kind you barely understood, "Nes' station, Mifford!" and went into the coach in front where, in the same train language, he made the same announcement.

The train was not crowded, so soon the conductor came back, sat down in his pop-up seat, wetted his forefinger, and counted the tickets he had. He made a note in his shiny black notebook. It made Jane happy to know that such a nice conductor knew, really *knew*, be it Ida or Ada, the name of the passenger opposite her, had it on his list.

She wished she had a little black notebook like his, all shiny and smelling of train, to write things in.

Jane took off her coat, folded it neatly, and laid it beside her. It did not take up much room. Supposing some new person getting on in "Mifford" wanted to sit beside her, there was room for both. She put her hat on top of her coat. Then she took out of her pocket the big fat timetable Joey had given her. She opened it up to the going to New York page, arriving and departing, found New Haven, found Cranbury, and put checks beside these. She was going to put a check beside every station they stopped at. If the next stop really was "Mifford," once and for all she would know she was on the right train. When she got home, she would return the timetable to Joey and say that you can believe what you see in print . . . at least if it is a timetable.

She looked out the window. Telegraph poles seemed to be falling like felled trees as the train whizzed by; then looking back, she could see them pop right side up again.

Sometimes the engineer blew a screaming warning whistle. That was when the train was approaching a country cross road that went right over the tracks with no gate or anything to warn people in carts or cars or on foot that a train was coming through. At one crossing a man with a wagon piled high with beautiful fresh vegetables sat by patiently waiting. His horse looked thin and tired and was probably glad to have a little rest.

Jane began to think about the lady opposite her. She had on a rusty black straw hat with a feather at the back. Jane already knew a few things about this lady, that she was named Ada

Brooks, that she had a ticket marked Greens Farms, and that she was going to visit a cousin there named Agnes. She was not what you would call a complete stranger.

Jane examined her big timetable. She found Greens Farms on the list . . . six stops from here. She and the lady were both, so far, on the right train. She smiled and, out of the corners of her eyes as Joey had instructed her, studied the lady more closely.

The lady was examining a little square wooden box filled with red raspberries. She fluffed them up a bit. Then she looked out her window. "Maybe," thought Jane, "she has been looking at me out of the corners of her eyes." She straightened her pretty blue dress.

Then she looked at the lady's box of raspberries, and she couldn't take her eyes off of it, for a little pale green inch worm was humping its way from berry to berry.

Jane did not like worms. Rufus did, and so did Nancy Stokes. Maybe the lady did not like worms either. Should she tell her? She knew the lady's name . . . Ada Brooks . . . so it would not be like speaking to a stranger. She could say it out of the corner of her mouth, while keeping her eyes straight ahead as Joey had advised, say, "Lady! There is a little green worm crawling on your raspberries!"

But suddenly, from across the aisle, a question was hurled at Jane loud enough to be heard above the clickety-clickety-clickety of the eight-fifteen.

"Girl!"

Jane jumped.

"Girl!" repeated the lady. "What's this train? Where's it going?"

This lady, Jane figured, needed to be reassured that she was on the right train, just the way Jane had had to have reassurance. Jane decided to answer this question hurled at her from across the aisle by a lady from Montowese where Mama had spent her honeymoon and started having hay fever. She would be daring; she would even look directly at her.

She said, "Lady. This is the eight-fifteen train from New Haven. It stopped at eight-twenty in Cranbury."

"Cranbury!" interrupted the lady. "Spell it . . . Cran*berry* or Cran*bury*?"

". . . ury. Cranbury," answered Jane, "where I got on. And next it will stop in Milford. The conductor just said so, even though he pronounces it 'Mifford.' So if it does stop in Milford, that will prove we are on the right train. After Milford it will go on and on and after many stops end up in Grand Central Station in New York City."

"New York!" gasped the lady. "Don't tell me! Perish the thought!"

"Yes," said Jane. "To Grand Central Station in New York. But you and me will not be on it . . . you getting off at Greens Farms and me in New Rochelle."

Jane opened up Joey's wonderful timetable. She leaned across the aisle. She ran her finger down the list of towns and cities the eight-fifteen was supposed to stop at. "There! You see? Greens Farms, where you get off, is five stops after Milford." There was a pause.

"Did someone put you on this train?" asked Jane.

"Walton did, my husband did, Walton did," answered the lady.

"Well," said Jane. "I guess that Walton is as good at remembering right trains as my brother Joey is. He remembers everything . . . right trains, right dates . . ."

"What do dates have to do with trains? Right train? Maybe. But maybe wrong date. Agnes said come on the fifteenth . . ."

"This is the fifteenth! Look at my ticket, look at yours . . . stamped August fifteenth," said Jane. The lady did.

"So far, so good," she said. She put a piece of chewing gum in her mouth and chewed slowly and thoughtfully. It smelled like double mint.

Then she said, "You see you threw me off showing me that paper you have there. Saying this train was on its way to New York! But first it will stop at Greens Farms. You would not lie. I can see by the look of you . . . you with your coat neatly folded and hat with cherries on top of it . . . that you would not lie to me. But Walton . . ."

The lady paused as though to make certain of this fact before uttering it. "Walton drove me to New Haven . . . the *Union* Station . . . no *Grand* about it . . . in his green wagon with a big sign, "FARM PRODUCE, THE BEST IN MONTOWESE," painted on it. Oh, he made Dobbin go fast, he did. And he put me on this train. I'm on my way to Greens Farms . . . raise Bermuda onions there. But look at the way we're whizzing along. The man who runs this train might be the sort that Walton is, whiz past a station for the fun of it. Walton might have put me on the wrong train, on the wrong date . . . anything, just for the fun of it. Not mean . . . just likes a little fun . . ."

"I don't think the New York, New Haven, & Hartford Railroad Company would have engineers that play jokes on passengers," said Jane.

"You noticed that cart standing still by the tracks so we could get past it? He had Bermuda onions in his cart, lots of 'em. That's what gave me the idea the engineer might have flown past Greens Farms, town of the Bermuda onions, for the fun of it . . ."

"Well," said Jane, and she had to laugh, "don't worry about that. Just worry about your raspberries. You've let some of them slide out of the box and onto the floor."

The lady gathered them up and fluffed them up, and Jane helped her, but she didn't see the worm. "Maybe gone back under, like a swimmer in a sea of raspberries," Jane thought.

For a while all was quiet. The conductor had come back to his seat, but did not sit down. He bellowed, "Mifford, Mifford nes' stop!"

Then he spoke to the lady from Montowese. "You don't get off here, ma'am. Not your station, Ida Brooks. I'll tell you when." Then he went in back and straddled the connecting platforms of this coach and the one behind.

"Did you hear him? There's no Ida Brooks on this train. I'm Ada, not Ida," she said. "We're identical twins."

"Well," said Jane, "everything will be all right. If you're identical twins, even Walton might a got mixed up!"

The lady chewed thoughtfully but said nothing.

"Don't worry," said Jane. "Your cousin Agnes probably loves both of you identically the same."

Now people were going to the doors with their packages and

satchels ready to get off, but not Jane, not the lady. Jane was excited. "What a train ride!" she thought. Everything was going as rehearsed in her conversation with Mrs. Price. "But same as in a play," she reminded herself, "something unexpected might happen, like the lady from Montowese and her green worm. If another unexpected thing happens, maybe more exciting, use your wits. Don't panic. Act as though that was the way things were meant to be."

Suddenly something did happen. The train came to a stop in the Milford station. Then there was excitement!

About fifty little boys and girls crowded onto the train, screaming, yelling, shouting, laughing. "I wanna seat by the window." It sounded like recess time at Wood Street School. They rushed to this side and that. They pushed one another out of a good spot and got into it themselves. Sometimes three sat one on top of another in a heap.

A minister . . . he must be a minister because he was dressed in a black suit and wore a stiff white collar backward around his neck like Ray Abbot . . . clapped his hands. "Children, children, behave. Be quiet!" He even blew a little whistle hoping to bring order.

"What's this?" Jane asked a little boy who slid into the seat beside her.

"Sunday School picnic," he said glumly, having been pushed

out of a good seat by a window and having to sit beside Jane instead. Jane put her coat and hat in her lap not to lose them in the confusion.

The minister was straddling the linkage between this coach and the one in front where some mothers and fathers had sat down and were hoping to take it easy.

All the children had brown paper bags with their lunches in them and bathing suits wrapped in towels. "What beach are you going to?" asked Jane.

"I forgotten," said the little boy forlornly.

Jane was sorry for him. He wanted to be in a heap along with a pile of children. He didn't want to sit by her. Jane looked across the aisle to see how the lady from Montowese was enjoying this picnic, but she couldn't see her. Three rather plump little girls were stacked up in the seat beside her, and they, with all their trappings, obscured Ada Brooks. But, ah, she must be there, for Jane did see the box of raspberries, which evidently she was holding high above on her black straw hat. It was lucky it was a flat hat. But Jane could not see the hat, so it looked as though the box of berries was afloat in the air.

"Poor lady!" thought Jane. "Too bad she didn't get this little thin boy instead of those three big girls piled in a heap beside her. How tired her arms must be holding her berries up high!"

Suddenly the conductor, whose wonderful little pop-up plush chair was now occupied by two little boys, appeared from in back. He said, "Nes' station, Devon! Devon, nes' station!"

The minister counted heads as best he could. He said, "Devon! That is where we get off. Gather your belongings together!"

The minister's announcement created a renewed frenzy of activity. Many dashed to the water fountain for one last drink and to get another paper cup, cone-shaped, to hold on their heads and say, "Clown! Clown! See, I'm a clown!" and pulled their mouths wide apart to make the grin of a sad clown. A few big girls had lipsticks and painted bright red circles on their cheeks. Some put their cups on their noses for a Pinocchio look.

"It's funny and pretty like a circus," Jane thought as the children pushed themselves out onto the platform, and they were gone.

The train did not start up right away. The children had to be counted again. There the minister was, looking haggard. But now he had some mothers and even fathers and older children to help him as he went down the list.

Jane looked across the aisle to see how the lady from Montowese had come through that onslaught.

She wasn't there! She and her raspberries were not there!

Her ticket was stuck where it was supposed to be, her satchel was beneath her seat, but no lady from Montowese!

Jane looked out the window, which was open as it had been all along. She spotted the lady, Ada Brooks, standing on the platform in the middle of the Sunday School picnic!

Jane shouted, "Hey, lady! Lady from Montowese! This is not your station! Get on! Get back on! Quick!"

The lady didn't hear her. She stood in the midst of the children, looking confused but clutching her raspberries as though they were a link between her and real life. The minister and the conductors were so busy counting children that no one heard Jane. They probably, if they did notice the lady from Montowese, thought she was somebody's grandmother . . . part of the picnic.

Only one thing for Jane to do! Get off this train, grab the lady by the arm, pull her to the steps of the train, and push her back on. So Jane got off.

"Ada! Ada Brooks!" Jane shouted.

Then the lady heard her name and pushed her way toward Jane. There was not such a huge throng left now, for special open trolley cars had been lined up to take the picnickers to where they were going.

The conductors, happy that those in charge of the picnic had accounted for all of the children, hopped back on the train, pulled the cord, ding-ding, toot-toot . . . and the train started up slowly. Chug . . . chug . . . puff . . . slow, fast, faster . . . and Jane and the lady from Montowese were left standing forlornly on the Devon railroad station where neither one of them was supposed to be. Satchels, tickets, coats, the lady's little towel she rested her head against . . . all were on the going-away train!

"I told you it was the wrong train," said the lady.

Jane paid no attention. She looked around. "Ah, there!" she cried. "Come on!" she said to the lady. "There's a trainman over there with a little handcar. Wait right here."

"I'm a statue," said the lady.

Jane ran over to the big man dressed in gray-striped overalls. "Man!" she said. "Me and this lady are supposed to be on that train that just left! I'm on my way to New Rochelle. The lady is going to Greens Farms. She got off by mistake with the picnic people, so I got off to get her back on, but too late! There goes our train, the eight-fifteen. Our tickets, our coats, our satchels, her head towel are on that train. What can we do?"

The man took in the situation right away. He lost no time. He got his little handcar from the siding, told Jane to hop on, which she did, then he hoisted the lady up and told her to hang onto her berries.

"I'll catch up with that train," he said, "because the draw-bridge across the Housatonic River is up for a stream of boats to go through. So don't worry! Your train will have to wait on this side for the boats. They line 'em up, big and little, and they go through the opening one by one."

"O-o-h!" said Jane in excitement. "We have one of those drawbridges in Cranbury, only it's just for trolleys, not trains . . ."

"Yeh, I know about that one . . . not for trains, though. Anyway," said the handcar man, "the engineer waits for all the boats to pass through. Then the drawbridge comes slowly back down, joins together again, tracks and all, and off the trains will go. Well, I'll go like sixty and catch up with your train . . . your eight-fifteen . . . and I'll get you back on!"

The man honked a horn, very loud. "Have to begin to get their attention as soon as possible, in case the bridge comes down before I make it." He honked and honked it. He let Jane honk it. It sounded important. And he pumped his nice flat little handcar lickety-split down the local tracks, chasing after the eight-fifteen.

"Wait till I tell Walton!" shouted the lady, who looked happy.

Way, way ahead, they could see the rear end of their train. Sure enough, it was beginning to slow down. "See, the bridge *is* up," observed the man. True! A big wall seemed to be rising up in front of the train. The eight-fifteen would have to stop or bump right smack into it, then fall onto the boats peacefully sailing through the opening toward Long Island Sound or up the beautiful Housatonic.

"What a river!" thought Jane. And what a ride she was having! She loved this little handcar. Wouldn't Joey and Rufus love being on this wonderful little handcar! She had been watching how the man made it go, pumping a rod up and down, up and down. It looked easy.

She said, "Mister Engineer, could I make the little car go? Just for a little while before we catch up with the eight-fifteen?"

"Sure, miss. But it's heavier than it looks. You take one end of the rod and I'll take the other, and we'll be a team!"

The engineer put a red bandanna handkerchief on Jane's hand so she wouldn't get a blister, and the two of them pumped the little handcar. It wasn't hard. Jane loved it! She laughed out loud. "Hey, mister, could I try it by myself?"

"Try it, but not for long. We don't want to miss that train!"

Jane stretched her thin arms from one end of the rod to the other, pressed it down, pulled it up, pressed it down, pulled it up. It wasn't easy. But wait till she told Mama and the boys, "I made a handcar go fast, real fast down the tracks to catch up with the eight-fifteen. Feel my muscle!" she'd say.

But she was tired and glad when the trainman took over completely because they would soon catch up with the train. He'd been counting the boats that had gone through, and there couldn't be many more.

"What's your name?" he asked.

"Jane," said Jane. "What's yours?"

"George," said the man. "Call me George."

"And call me Ada, not Ida," said the lady from Montowese

who, clutching her berries, was perched precariously at the edge of the handcar. She looked happy. "Wait till I tell Walton!" she said. "And Agnes!"

"We have to hurry now," George said. He pumped harder and harder. Jane honked his horn . . . honk, honk . . . constantly.

"Wait for Ada!" screamed the lady from Montowese.

They could see the drawbridge. It was beginning to come down. Would they make it? Fortunately, two conductors smoking their pipes on the rear platform spotted the oncoming handcar with people aboard. One ran into the back car and pulled the emergency cord. This made a screaming whistle that meant, "Motorman, stop! Put on the brakes!" Jane put her hands over her ears. She bet they could hear that whistle way back in Cranbury, and all the fire engines would come roaring out.

But no, the train, which had started slowly, stopped with a sudden lurch. A conductor with a megaphone such as they have in baseball fields bellowed into it.

"Passengers! Don't worry. This is not a wreck. Missing passengers arriving by handcar. Got lost somehow or other along the line!"

George pumped his handcar as close to the rear of the train as he could, letting Jane have the last swing at it. Then he lifted Jane over the back railing of the train, the conductor grabbed her, and she was on! Then George lifted the frail little lady from Montowese up, and the conductor grabbed her, too.

"Don't lose my berries!" she warned. Miraculously, he didn't.

"George!" Jane called out to her friend, the handcar engineer. "Thank you! Thank you! I'll send you a Christmas card. Where do I send it?"

The train was pulling out now. The conductor had rung the "All clear" signal. But Jane heard George shout, "Just put 'George, the handcar man, New York, New Haven, & Hartford Railroad Company.' I'll get it. Everybody knows George!"

"O-o-oh," screamed Jane. "I have your bandanna!"

"Keep it!" said George. "Souvenir!"

"Thank you! Thank you," she shouted. "I'll put it in the museum . . . The Moffat Museum!"

"Good . . . good . . ." he said.

Now Jane could barely hear him. He had swung his rod over. The handcar could go backward or forward with a switch of the rod. He turned. He waved. He honked his horn and started pumping his way back to the Devon station. Jane waved his bandanna as long as she could see him. Then the conductor hustled Jane back into her same seat and the lady from Montowese into hers.

No one had taken anything. Jane's coat, her hat with the cherries, and her satchel were exactly where she had left them.

Her ticket stamped New Rochelle was still in its little slot.

Across the aisle, the lady from Montowese was counting her belongings. She straightened her rumpled little head towel and examined it closely. "For lice," she explained to Jane. She sat down, rested her head against her little towel, fluffed up her berries, and made the box seem full. Then she popped one in her mouth. She even offered one to Jane.

"No, thank you," said Jane, though she was hungry. Where was the worm? she wondered.

Now the time passed quickly. The train went very fast to make up for time lost at the drawbridge over the Housatonic. It seemed to Jane she scarcely had time to put a check on her timetable by the name of one station before they were at the next.

Suddenly the conductor hopped up from his pop-up seat and said, "Greens Farms! Station, Greens Farms!"

Jane watched the lady gather up her belongings. She said, "I hope you have a nice visit."

This brought a smile to the lady's face. She said, "You're a right smart little girl, running that contraption up the tracks. And all the while we were on the right train until then. Oh, Walton, oh, he can be mean, but he wouldn't do a thing like that, put me on the wrong train. I hope you're on your right one and that paper you have there is to be trusted. Otherwise, hop off and get yourself onto one of those little contraptions again and pump it down the tracks to Neufchâtel."

"New Rochelle," Jane said. "Neufchâtel's a cheese. We eat it . . . snappy!"

"Cheese! Now, I've heard everything," said the lady.

The conductor came up to the Montowese lady. He said, "Come on, Ida Brooks. You get off here. This is Greens Farms. No more excursions on handcars this trip."

He took her satchel, but she hung onto her raspberries. Jane watched her from the window. A jolly-looking rather plump lady rushed to meet her. "That must be Agnes," thought Jane.

"Ada!" screamed Agnes. She laughed heartily. "Ada! Of all things! I thought Ida was coming. What a nice surprise! I love Ida and I love you!" She kissed and hugged Ada some more to prove this. Ada smiled and handed her the raspberries.

The train began to move. The last thing Jane heard the lady from Montowese say was, "Oh, dear me! Oh, deary me! Did you write 'Ida' not 'Ada'? Your writing is so bad. Oh, I am the wrong person . . ."

Jane heard no more, but looking back out the open window, she saw Ada making motions as though making a little handcar go, pushing the imaginary rod up and pressing down, and pointing back down the tracks while a look of marvel spread over Agnes's face. Then suddenly remembering Jane, her rescuer, the lady pointed Jane out to her cousin. Both waved, and that was the last Jane saw of that lady from Montowese.

Peace now on the eight-fifteen. A major unexpected happening that had not been rehearsed had happened. Would there be more?

A man sat down in Ada's seat. Then he noticed a little green worm inching its way along the windowsill, raising its head now and then as though to get its bearings. Little did he know this was a traveler worm that had been on a handcar in a box of berries. When the worm reached the end of the sill and paused in its searching, the man gently lifted it between his thumb and forefinger and dropped it out the window.

"What a kind man!" thought Jane. "And how brave! To pick up a little lost worm! I'll learn to be that brave sometime . . ."

Jane checked Greens Farms off on her timetable. She examined George's red bandanna, folded it carefully, and put it in her pocket. She smiled. It had "N.Y., N.H., & H. R.R. Co." printed on it in white. What an addition to the museum!

Then dreamily she watched the passing scene, almost forgetting to mark off the stops . . . hills in the far places, small rivers meandering . . .

She came to with a start. "Nes' station, New Rochelle!" said the conductor. Jane quickly gathered her things together and stood up and went to the back of the coach to stand beside the conductor.

He recognized her as the little girl who had rescued a little lost lady and had propelled a handcar lickety-lickety down the tracks to catch up with the eight-fifteen.

"Goin' by handcar wherever you're goin'?" he joked as he helped her off.

Jane smiled. "Nope!" she said. "Don't know yet . . ."

And that was the last that Jane saw of that nice conductor or the eight-fifteen as it started up and went puff-puff-puffing on its way to Grand Central Station, New York.

Jane stood on the platform to get her bearings. She looked around. She knew what trolley she should take if Ray and Sylvie did not meet her, or that she could walk.

She didn't see Ray and Sylvie. She did see the trolley, but she had just decided to walk when she heard a familiar horn . . . sounded just like Sam Doody's horn. And there were Ray and Sylvie riding up to the curb, waving, saying, "Jane! Jane! We're a little late. But here we are!"

So she had after all been met by Ray and Sylvie and been driven to their home in Wheezy.

It wasn't far. They passed the little wooden church, where

Ray was the minister. Right next to it was their house, the rectory, brown like the church. They drove around a few blocks so Jane would know where some stores were and where she was at if she went for a walk, and she saw some nice little shops and thought she would buy a present for Joey and Rufus some time when she didn't have anything to do.

But there wasn't going to be much of that. The week flew by. It seemed as though the ride on the eight-fifteen was longer than the whole week that she stayed with Sylvie and Ray.

The first thing they did was have a big dinner of Swedish meatballs and other good things. They were very interested in Jane's story of the ride on the little handcar and all about the lady from Montowese. They both knew Montowese well themselves and felt a little homesick sometimes for those picnics they used to have up on Peter's Rock. The confusion about Ada and Ida made Ray burst into guffaws.

After dinner Ray went into his study to work on his sermon, and Sylvie said she had to go and meet with the Girls' Friendly but would not be long. It was like that every day. It might just as well have been Cranbury, for Sylvie was always having choir rehearsals, altar guild meetings, sewing circle meetings, and suchlike.

Although Sylvie did teach Jane how to crochet and to embroider, so that Jane was able to put lace around a little hand-kerchief for Mama, Jane found she did have some time to herself, to read, to sew, and to go for walks.

The first walk she took was to the row of small shops. In the window of one she had seen little shiny black leather notebooks like the trainman and the conductor had to write important train matters in.

She bought three . . . one for Joey for his dates and facts and figures, even though he really didn't need to write these things down. He had them in his head. Jane didn't know what Rufus would put in his, but she knew what she would put in hers . . . "Conversations." That was going to be the name of her note-book.

When she got back in her little room after her walk, she rubbed all the notebooks on the bandanna that George had given her, so when she got home to Cranbury, she could say, "Smell them. What do they smell like?"

If they didn't know, she would say, "Train."

And so the week went by. Oh yes, they took some rides in Wheezy, one lovely one along a river on a new parkway and one to an amusement park in Rye. But before she knew it, she was back in Wheezy with Sylvie and Ray going to the railroad station. This time it was a train in the early afternoon, a two

o'clock train from Grand Central so that she would be home in time for dinner.

"Give my love to Mama. Give my love to everybody," said Sylvie. As the train was leaving, she was trying not to cry.

Soon Jane was back in Cranbury. Joey was there at the station. At dinner she told them about Ray and Sylvie and how they lived. But the story they wanted to have her tell again and again was how she and a little lady from Montowese had a ride on a handcar to catch up with their train. And they all liked the part about the raspberries and the little green worm.

"Montowese! Montowese!" Mama murmured, for many memories lay behind that name.

Mama admired the handkerchief. Joey loved the notebook, rubbed it, thought he might work for that railroad company some day. Rufus rushed up to his room with his leather notebook and right away wrote in it the words: TROLLEY CARS.

The next morning Jane climbed the fence. She hoped it was laundry day for Mrs. Price. It was. Mrs. Price came out with her basket.

"Jane, you back? So soon? How was it all? Come over here."

Jane jumped down. She and Mrs. Price sat on the back stoop. Jane began her story. "Well, there was a lady on the train . . ."

"Do tell! I want to know," said Mrs. Price. So Jane told her the story of her ride on the eight-fifteen.

"You know?" she said. "It was just exactly like I said. You can rehearse and rehearse a play or a happening. But the real thing is never exactly the way you had it all rehearsed in your mind."

"I know," said Mrs. Price, nodding her head sagely. "Who would ever have thought up a handcar?"

8

THE ONE-DOLLAR TROLLEY CAR

ONE SATURDAY MORNING RUFUS WAS SITTING BY HIMSELF
on the curbstone at the corner of Ashbellows Place and Elm
Street watching the trolley cars go by. He was feeling a little
lonesome, but the sight of the trolley cars going back and forth
cheered him up. They made him think of the carbarn. In all

of Cranbury, the carbarn was his and Joey's favorite place to visit.

On Saturday mornings they had almost always gone over to the carbarn to look at the trolleys, but this summer Joey had so many jobs to do that he couldn't spend Saturday mornings in the carbarn.

The carbarn was deep and wide and filled with tracks and switches and trolley cars. The trolleys waiting to go out were near the front. Some with workmen under them or in them, fixing something, were near the back. But it wasn't these trolleys that drew Joey and Rufus like a magnet to the carbarn.

Way, way back, in the very darkest and dustiest corner of the carbarn, was one little trolley car only about one quarter the length of regular ones. It was not a toy. It was a real trolley car, short but just as high, and it had its own pole to guide it on the wires overhead.

It was a closed-in trolley car, not one of the open summertime ones. Joey and Rufus always made their way immediately to that little trolley car, stared at it and studied it. They loved it. They wished they owned it. From the time Rufus was a very little boy, Joey had taken him to see that little trolley. It was always right there in that back corner, as though expecting visitors, them . . . Joey and Rufus. Once Rufus told Joey he thought he had seen it in the distance going down Elm Street. He wasn't sure. Joey was skeptical. But then, thinking it over, Joey said, "Well, maybe they do take it out once in a while at odd times, maybe even in the nighttime, to make sure it could still run if it had to."

They never checked with any of the men who worked in the carbarn, all of whom had gotten to know Joey and Rufus. They just liked to imagine things like this about the little trolley car, and at night in bed sometimes they made up stories about it, some very funny, and they laughed themselves to sleep and dreamed about the little trolley.

If the men in the carbarn ever did take the little trolley out, Rufus thought this might be the very day. They might run it down Elm Street right past him, to check and see if it could be a useful trolley again.

No such thing happened. Rufus had a powerful craving to see the little trolley, but he'd never been to the carbarn without Joey. Joey was helping Mrs. Crowley trim the show windows of her department store opposite the green, not far from the carbarn. He was probably putting down fresh crinkly crepe paper, pads and pencils, straw hats, maybe. He was probably wishing the same thing Rufus was, that he could take a look at their little trolley. They had gotten to call it theirs. It was a shame to have it just stand there dusty and forsaken. All the other trolleys, the closed-in ones and the open ones, went in and out, but not that one-and-only small one.

It should belong to people like him and Joey who'd take good care of it, thought Rufus. It shouldn't just stay back there; it looked lonesome and anxious to get out on the tracks again.

"Maybe I should go there by myself and take a look at it, make sure it hasn't been stolen . . . or bought," thought Rufus. "Why shouldn't I go there alone?" he asked himself. He'd wave to Joey if he was in the show window. Joey would know where he was going . . . to the carbarn!

The carbarn was practically catty-corner from Crowley's. It was next to a small graveyard with ancient gravestones, slim slabs of granite bending forward from severe storms.

Rufus stood up. He decided to take the short cut across the empty lot behind the library and run down Campbell Avenue, wave to Joey if he did see him, then cross the street and race over to the carbarn. The man in the little office in the front would let him come in; he knew Rufus and Joey very well. He was nice and always said, "Hello." He was used to seeing Rufus with his older brother, but Rufus thought he would let him in, that he knew he could trust Rufus by himself or with anybody else, a friend perhaps. He was the man in charge of the comings and goings of all trolleys, see that they had the right signs on them, that they were spick and span. The carbarn was like a stable, only it was filled with trolley cars, not horses.

About to take off on this expedition, Rufus stopped. Along came his friend Uncle Bennie Pye. Uncle Bennie was famous in Cranbury because, as far as anyone knew, he was the only inhabitant who had been born an uncle. Rachel and Jerry Pye, a girl and a boy about Jane's age, were his niece and his nephew.

Uncle Bennie lived on the other side of town, near Sandy Beach, and he didn't go to the same school as Rufus. But often on Saturday he came over this way to visit Rachel and Jerry, where he was allowed to walk their smart dog, Ginger, heaving and gasping on his hated leash.

Sometimes Jerry and Rachel didn't want to play with their little uncle. They wanted to play with older friends. So sometimes Uncle Bennie, like Rufus, felt a little lonesome on Saturdays and often came to The Moffat Museum. He and Rufus had therefore struck up a sort of a Saturday-morning friendship. Helping Rufus strew petals down on Sylvie at her wedding had cemented this friendship.

To please this occasional visitor to the museum, Rufus sometimes put on his waxworks face and became a Madame Tussaud statue for Uncle Bennie. But then he got tired of being a waxworks person for just one visitor, and without asking Jane or Joey could he or couldn't he, he put an extra sign on the museum. It said in colossal letters: OUT FOR LUNCH.

So now, when Rufus saw his friend Uncle Bennie coming along Elm Street, he sat down again. He moved over so Bennie could sit beside him and not have a huge elm tree obstruct his friend's view of the trolleys as they came along.

They both said, "Hello!" Then they sat in silence getting used to being together again. Trolleys came and went. Sometimes a motorman or a conductor waved at the boys. Many knew Rufus because he had visited the carbarn so often.

"Bennie," said Rufus, "have you ever been to the carbarn?"

Bennie shook his head. "No," he said.

"Well, Bennie," said Rufus, "how would you like to go to the carbarn with me now? It should be on Mr. Pennypepper's annual tour. It's the best place in town."

Ashamed of his ignorance, Bennie said, "I bet it is."

"Well, you want to come with me or not?" said Rufus, standing up.

"Will we be back by twelve?" asked Bennie. "I always have to be back by twelve."

"Sure," said Rufus. "We have the twelve o'clock rule in my house, too. The clock on the green rings at twelve. We'll tear home then."

The two boys started off. Bennie was only a year younger

than Rufus, but he seemed much smaller. Rufus was proud to be the big one of the expedition. "I'm taking Joey's place," he thought. But he had better do a little explaining.

He said, "Bennie, I'll tell you why the carbarn is so great. All carbarns all over the world are probably great, but this Cranbury one is probably the greatest of all. Way, way in the back of it, in the dark and dusty back of it, on a short track all its own is a little trolley car, one of the closed-in kind, like the Bridgeport Express. But this little trolley car is only about one-quarter the length of a regular closed-in trolley. Just as wide, just as high, has a pole on top for the wires, but it's just plain short. It's not a toy. It could go anywhere, but it doesn't. It just stays there in the barn all the time."

"Not a toy. Just short, just plain short," repeated Bennie.

"Yes," said Rufus. "Me and Joey wish we could buy this little trolley car, wash it . . . it's a little sooty . . . run it down Elm Street, switch it onto Second Avenue, maybe, and run it up that street."

"That's my line," said Bennie. "The new Second Avenue line . . . it gets you there on time."

Rufus laughed. They sang the song together. Then Rufus said, "If we ever get to own it and run it up the new Second Avenue line, Joey and me will let you stand at the steering wheel, and I'll stomp on the pedal and make it go ding-ding-

ding when we pass your corner. We'll wave to people we know and people we don't know. They will be astonished at the sight of a trolley that little coming up their street."

"It's sort of like a pet," said Bennie.

"You're right," said Rufus. "It is Joey's and my pet trolley. Joey and me would take turns, him being the motorman, me the conductor, or vice versa," said Rufus.

"What's vice versa?" asked Bennie. "Are you a foreigner?"

"Nope. I was born on New Dollar Street. Vice versa means one or t'other. This trolley can seat only about twelve. We'd take mainly kids unless, of course, it was someone like Judge Bell. He lives on Second Avenue. We'd give him a ride."

"He's so tall," said Bennie. "Could he fit in?"

"Sure, once he sits down. He has to do that on a regular trolley, too . . . has to stoop until he sits down. I told you this is like a regular trolley, just small!" said Rufus.

The two boys were opposite the green now, nearing Crowley's Department Store. Rufus said, "Bennie. Walk a little in front of me. Don't look in the show window. Joey doesn't like to have people stare at him if he happens to be in it decoratin'."

Uncle Bennie walked past Crowley's Department Store straight as a ramrod and without a single glance at it. It was as though his eyes were focused on an unusual occurrence far ahead.

Rufus paused in front of the show window where Joey was crouching down and arranging pads and pencils and toy pails and shovels, straw hats, many sorts of things, and he was being careful not to get himself stuck in the fresh curls of flypaper he had suspended from the ceiling. He spotted Rufus and raised his eyebrows, meaning what's up?

Rufus pointed ahead at Uncle Bennie striding stiffly on. Then Rufus jerked his head toward the carbarn. This meant was it O.K. to take Uncle Bennie to the carbarn to see their little trolley car? Joey nodded. It was O.K.

Rufus caught up with Bennie in front of Moose Hall. They crossed the street, walked past the ancient graveyard, grass uncut, wisps of pretty weeds, some with pale blue or yellow flowers, growing haphazardly here and there.

But now, here now, was the carbarn!

Before going in, Rufus did a little explaining to Uncle Bennie. He showed him how the switches had to be shunted this way or that so the trolleys would lurch themselves onto the right track—some to Savin Rock or some, vice versa, to New Haven or Lighthouse Point maybe, which was exactly opposite Cranbury on the other side of the harbor.

Rufus said, "You don't have to go to one or the other of those places. If you didn't want to get off at some street on the way, you could get transfers and take a long trip. You could get all the way to Boston, Chicago maybe, almost never have to pay another nickel . . . just one transfer after another and maybe land in Limerick, Maine. Who knows? If me and Joey could only just buy our little trolley, that's what we might do, run it on long trips, not just up the Second Avenue trolley line. Maybe you could come, too."

"Bring my pajamas," said Bennie. "Sleep on a trolley car!"

They stood aside because a trolley was coming out. The motorman adjusted the switch, and the trolley turned down the way the boys had come. The sign in front said: MONTOWESE.

"Might be just the start of its plan to join up with another trolley and head, like you said, for Limerick, Maine," said Bennie, awestricken at all he was learning, and not even in school! Just from his good friend, Rufus Moffat!

"Who knows?" said Rufus. "But come on in."

There was a little office facing all the switches outside. A tall man was sitting on a high stool at a slanting desk, notebook in front of him. "He is the boss man of the whole carbarn," Rufus whispered to Bennie. "Tells a car when to go out, sees that another comes in when it's supposed to. His name is on his hat, Captain Moody."

Captain Moody said, "Hello, Rufus. Where's Joey?"

"Workin'," said Rufus. "I brought my friend instead to show him the carbarn. He's never been in it before! His name is Uncle Bennie Pye."

"O.K.," said Captain Moody. "Welcome to the Cranbury carbarn, home of the Connecticut Company's finest and best."

The boys laughed and went on in. They walked slowly through it. Rufus wanted to make the approach to the deep, dusky rear last a long time. He pointed out this trolley or that, the closed ones, the open ones. He told Uncle Bennie to look up and see how funny the pigeons atop the dusty dome-shaped glass roof looked from down below.

"Pigeons!" murmured Uncle Bennie. "I'll tell Rachel's father —he's a bird man, you know. Pigeons on a glass carbarn roof!"

"They come in when it rains. The men don't mind. They coo up there in the rafters," said Rufus.

They were way, way in the back now. "Bennie," said Rufus. "Give me your hand and close your eyes. You are going to see something as valuable as anything they have in the Smithsonian Institution."

Bennie gave Rufus his hand. He closed his eyes as tightly as he could. He felt his way carefully with his feet, not to step on an important thing. In a short while they had reached their destination, the dark and shadowy corner where the little trolley car stayed.

"Now, Bennie," Rufus said triumphantly, "open your eyes!"

Bennie opened his eyes, clasped his hands together, and gasped.

"That's it!" said Rufus.

"Oh, gosh!" said Bennie. "Oh, golly!"

"What'd I tell you?" said Rufus. "You like it?"

"Like it!" said Bennie. "I love this little trolley car!"

"Me and Joey, too," said Rufus happily. "We both of us love this trolley. We call it *our* little trolley car. If we could really own it, you could help us a lot. Be the switchman, sometimes. Even sit on the motorman's chair, if Joey would let you. And you know my brother, Joey! He'd let you!"

Uncle Bennie was speechless. To think that all of this could happen on a Saturday morning because he had a friend like Rufus.

Rufus studied Bennie's radiant face. He knew now for certain that he had a real friend who liked the same things that he and Joey liked.

"It never goes out," said Rufus. "Always stays right here. Joey and me pretend we own it, him the motorman, me the conductor. We take turns. We punch tickets, give out transfers.

I mean, we have all these in our pockets. Captain Moody gave us a lot of old used ones."

"Ever been inside it?" asked Bennie.

"Not yet, but probably some day . . ." said Rufus.

They stooped down and looked under the trolley, the way two men nearby were doing to their big trolley. They couldn't see much. Outside it was warm and sunny. Inside it was dim and dusky. The two men working on the big trolley carried a lantern so they could get a good look at the underneath part.

But Rufus and Bennie didn't have a lantern and stood up. Because this was Bennie's first visit to the carbarn, he had a great deal to take in, and Rufus saw to it that he saw everything.

Wan sunshine filtered through the rounded glass roof, which may never have been washed except by rain from the day long ago when it had been built. But the filmy sunlight barely seeping through lent a dreamy magic to the golden trolleys within, especially to the little one in the corner, not used, just there to be admired, first by Joey and Rufus, and now by Rufus and Uncle Bennie . . . the trolley they longed to have.

They stood on tiptoe to look through one of the windows. The little trolley had only four on each side . . . but the boys were too little to see in. "Climb up on my shoulders," said Rufus, "and see what you can see."

Bennie was just about to do this when a workman with a sooty lantern came out from under the trolley he was examining, a closed-in one like the little trolley car. Bennie slid off of Rufus's back and stood close to Rufus in case it was against the rules to look inside the little trolley car.

Rufus knew this man. It was Jim Cullom, brother of Spec Cullom, the iceman. Long ago Joey and Rufus had had conversations about trolleys with him. He was nice. Now he said, "You two fellas want to sit in the little trolley car?"

Speechless, Rufus and Bennie could only nod their heads. The answer was written all over their shining faces.

Jim Cullom opened the door with a special key that could probably open any closed-in trolley in the United States and maybe Canada. He gave Bennie a boost up the high step. Rufus had already climbed in. Jim Cullom went away with his lantern to some other trolley car.

The boys began their complete examination of everything . . . all the workings of this perfect little trolley car. It should be a *used* trolley car, not one stuck away in a corner doing nothing. There was its switch so that it could go on any trolley line. It hung on a strong iron hook beside the motorman's seat. At each end of the trolley there was a place for the motorman to sit. His seat was not much bigger than the seat of a bike and was removable. Take it off one end of the trolley and put it on the other. Never have to turn the trolley around. Its front could be its back or its back could be its front.

"Wasn't that smart, whoever thought that up?" marveled Rufus. Also in front and in back on the floor there was a brass bell that the motorman could pound his foot on to warn someone to get out of the way. If he got mad at a lazy dog or whatever was holding him up, he could stand up and stomp, stomp, stomp on the bell in the floor.

Rufus stepped on it, but it didn't ring. "Needs polishing," he said. "Or maybe it doesn't ring unless the trolley is connected to the wire."

Bennie smiled. He had a friend who knew so much!

Soon they felt they knew everything about this trolley car. There were even straps to hang onto, just like regular big trolleys. There were two radiators for heat, one on each side. They could sleep in this trolley, live in it, but best of all, just have it for around Cranbury, go here and there, get listed on Captain Moody's schedule so nothing like the Bridgeport Express would come clanging along behind them and make them shift over to another track in a big hurry!

When they got out, they would see what it looked like underneath; maybe that nice Jim Cullom would hold his lantern down there so they could take a look. Just then Jim

Cullom and another workman Rufus had never seen before came back with their black-tin lunch boxes. Rufus and Uncle Bennie opened the door themselves and hopped down.

Jim Cullom sat down with his friend on the running board of an open trolley near the little trolley. They opened their lunch boxes. They put their lantern down beside them, and it cast some light under the little trolley car.

Now Rufus and Bennie had seen everything.

It was time for Rufus to speak. "Mr. Cullom," he said, "me and my friend Ben Pye and my brother, Joey . . . you know him, you know me . . . well, we would like to buy this little old trolley car that nobody uses any more. Joey and me have been watching it for a long long time. It never goes out. We'd like to buy it and take it out once in a while."

The second man said, "H-m-m. Want to buy this little old trolley car?"

"Yes, mister. Could we? How much does it cost?"

"Cost . . . ? Well-ll, lessee," said that second man. "One dollar!"

Rufus and Bennie were surprised. A dollar is a lot of money for something nobody uses. Before Rufus could answer, that new man and Jim Cullom walked off, laughing. "Ha-ha-ha!" echoed throughout the big carbarn and to the back corner where Rufus and Bennie, stunned at such a piece of good news, were standing.

Rufus was a little puzzled. Why were they laughing? Oh, now he had it. It struck them funny that anybody would want to buy what they thought so little of that they stuck it in the farthest, darkest corner of the carbarn.

Rufus and Bennie tore after the men and caught up with them. Rufus said, "Don't sell it to anybody else. Keep it for us. We'll be back with the dollar as soon as we can. Don't let anybody know, don't show it . . ."

"Oh, no!" said the new man. "Oh, no! We won't tell a living soul. One dollar and it's yours . . ."

The two men sat down on the running board of an open trolley and lighted their pipes. They didn't even look up and wave as Rufus and Bennie tore past them and out!

They ran down the street. Maybe Joey was still in the show window. Breathlessly Rufus said, "Joey and me always knew that someday we would own that little trolley car. Wait till he hears! Maybe by now he has earned a dollar or saved it or something. A dollar's a lot ...!"

"Same price the Pyes paid for Ginger," said Uncle Bennie. "Rachel and Jerry's dog, Ginger ... Ginger Pye."

"And was *he* ever worth it!" exclaimed Rufus. "What a dog!"

"What a dog is right!" said Bennie.

"We'll take him for a ride sometimes," panted Rufus.

"He'll love it ... loves to ride in cars, Sam Doody's ..." panted Bennie.

"When me and Joey own it, our little trolley car, you can be our special helper, our right-hand man. You can do anything, Bennie," said Rufus.

"Gee, thanks," said Bennie.

When they reached Crowley's Department Store, Joey was just coming out. Rufus saw Mrs. Crowley hand Joey something, money probably ... Joey's pay. "Thank you, Joey," she said and closed the screen door fast not to let a fly in.

Now! Now Rufus could tell Joey the great news!

Joey folded the bill ... Rufus saw that it was a crisp new one ... and he put it in his pants pocket.

"How much did the lady pay you?" asked Rufus.

"One dollar," said Joey. "Twenty-five cents a week. She owed me for four weeks."

Rufus was stupefied. One dollar equals one little trolley car! Finally he spoke. "Great news, Joey! Great news! Great news! But we better sit on the bench on the green. We don't want any spies around listening."

They sat down on a bench.

"Listen, Joey! You saw Bennie and me going to the carbarn. I showed him all over the barn, the trolleys, the switches . . . I was leading slowly up to the you know what . . ."

"The little trolley car . . . *our* little trolley car," said Joey, smiling.

"Listen to this then," said Rufus. "That nice man, Jim Cullom . . . remember him, brother of the iceman? . . . well, he came out from under a trolley and saw Bennie and me admirin' the trolley. You know what he said? He said we could sit in it, 'xamine it from the inside. He unlocked the door with a special key . . . we'll probably have one some day . . . and we got in. We 'xamined everything. We know how everything works. We could all ride it down to Savin Rock right now, will, when . . ."

"That must have been nice," said Joey. "I never *sat* in it."

"You will! You will. Listen. Pretty soon that nice man named Jim Cullom came along with another man. They sat down on the running board of an open trolley near our little one and opened their lunch boxes. That was when I asked the men if my brother Joey and I could buy the little trolley car that sits in the back of the carbarn and never goes anywhere?

"The new man didn't think it over at all. Right away he said he'd sell it to us."

"He did?" said Joey incredulously. "Why didn't we ever ask before?"

"Never had the nerve. So then I asked, 'How much does it cost?' I thought he would say ten dollars at least. But no! Guess!"

"A hundred?" guessed Joey.

"No!" said Rufus triumphantly. "ONE DOLLAR!"

"ONE DOLLAR!" repeated Joey. "You're kiddin'."

"I'm not kiddin'," said Rufus. "Am I kiddin', Bennie?"

Bennie solemnly shook his head.

"Sitting there on the running board of the open trolley car, that new man said we could buy it for a dollar. Jim Cullom didn't say anything. Maybe he was just thinkin', thinkin' he might miss the little trolley."

Joey reached in his pocket. He took out his crisp new one-dollar bill. Rufus could hear how it crinkled as he folded it more tightly. "Here!" he said, as though he were John D. Rockefeller. "Take this dollar and buy our little trolley car!"

Rufus took the dollar, all tightly folded, and put it in a little pocket in his khaki shorts that had a button on it which he rarely used, but he did now all right. "I'll pay my share when I can earn it, or find it," said Rufus.

"You'd'a thought somebody else would have bought it long ago," mused Joey.

"Probably nobody but us noticed it, or maybe they didn't have a dollar, or maybe they didn't know how to make it go," said Rufus. "But we know everything, don't we, Bennie?"

Bennie nodded and smiled. "Yes," he said. "Even underneath parts."

Rufus and Joey had not forgotten about Uncle Bennie. Should they let Bennie be a partner? But the little trolley had always been Joey and Rufus's.

Rufus knew what to do. "Bennie," said Rufus. "Since you have sat in Joey's and my little trolley car, you can be our one and only crew man. You can polish the clanger, turn the switch in the tracks sometimes, sweep up after we take a little trip . . . lots of things . . ."

Bennie was delighted. "Wait till I tell Rachel and Jerry, and Ma and Pa!" he said. "I like to polish."

"We'll let them have a ride once in a while, and Jane. Just special people, who know not to drop chewing gum on the floor or stick it under the seat."

"Where we going to keep our trolley car?" asked Joey. "No tracks on Ashbellows Place."

"Don't worry, Joey," said Rufus. "When I hand over the dollar and the trolley belongs to us, I'll ask those nice men if the little trolley can stay, except when we take it out for a little ride, right where it's always been. Except they will have to put a sign on front saying something. We'll think what . . . maybe SPECIAL!"

Joey laughed. "*Special* all right. And sounds sensible. I wish I could come along when you hand over the dollar, but I can't. Have to mow a couple of lawns. Remember to have something in writing, Rufus, saying we are the owners . . . a receipt for the dollar. Bye!"

Joey swung himself onto his bike, rang the bell three times, and sped away.

Rufus looked after him. He wished Joey could have come, too. "We won't ever take it out without Joey. Right, Bennie?"

"Right," said Bennie. "But," he said, "we have to hurry. Someone might come along and say he would give them two dollars, even three . . . five!"

"The man said he would hold it for us," said Rufus. "All day."

"And he was a nice man," said Bennie. "Gave me a bite of his pickle."

They took a drink at the drinking trough on the corner of the green. Revived, they raced back to the carbarn. At first they couldn't spot the two nice men. They went way to the back of the carbarn. There the little trolley car was, just waiting for them!

Where were those nice men? At last! One came out from under one trolley, the other from another trolley. They sat down again on the running board of the open trolley car where the big business had been arranged. The men mopped their faces with red handkerchiefs, for they were sooty and grimy and smelled of oil.

Jim Cullom and his friend told one funny joke after another. They laughed a great deal, each one trying to be funnier than the other. They didn't notice Rufus and Uncle Bennie standing nearby.

"Come on, Bennie. We have to give them the dollar now. They might go away," Rufus said. Bennie nodded.

"We have the dollar, Mr. Cullom," said Rufus. "To pay for the little trolley car." He and Bennie put loving hands on the side of their trolley. Rufus undid the button of his little square pocket and got out the dollar bill.

There was a silence. The men looked at Rufus and at Bennie and at the crisp new dollar bill. They didn't say anything. They stared, half amused, half puzzled. They didn't seem to know what to say.

Rufus held out Joey's dollar bill, carefully unfolded it, and showed it to the men so they could see it was not a counterfeit or a toy bill from a money game.

"See?" said Rufus. "Here's the dollar. We said we'd be back. So now me and Joey and Bennie can take it out sometimes if you will let us keep it here, right here where it's used to being."

The men remained silent. Neither of them reached out for Rufus's dollar.

"Well?" said Rufus. "Here's the dollar. Joey asked me to get a receipt."

Jim Cullom said nothing. He rubbed the sole of his heavy black shoe back and forth on the sandy part next to the tracks. Finally he said, "Bill?"

The new man, Bill, said, "Aw, kids! I was jokin'."

"Jokin'!" said Rufus. "Just jokin'!"

The man didn't answer. He nodded his head.

Jim Cullom didn't look at Rufus at all. He bent over and tied his shoelaces tighter.

Rufus and Bennie tore out of the carbarn and all the way home to the Moffats' house. They sat down on the curb under the big elm tree in front. They were waiting for Joey, who came along in a few minutes. Rufus handed Joey his crisp Crowley one-dollar bill.

"The guy said he was just jokin'," said Rufus.

Joey folded his dollar neatly again and put it back in his pocket. He said, "People should not play jokes."

"Only in the funny papers," said Uncle Bennie.

Joey was silent for a moment, looking at Rufus. He said, "Well, we can still call it 'our' trolley car. We can go and look at it. Me and you and Bennie can go . . . whenever we want, still *wish* it was ours, like always."

Rufus said, "Maybe we should go back . . . me and *you*, Joey. Maybe they thought they shouldn't sell it to fellows as little as me and Uncle Bennie. But you! You have a suit with long pants. Put it on and let's go back."

"Naw!" said Joey. "They really were just jokin'. And I can't go now. I still have one more lawn to mow." Joey rode away.

He couldn't help it. Rufus began to cry a little. Tears made a clean line down his cheeks. Bennie pretended not to notice and bowed his head in sadness.

But someone had noticed. This was the iceman, Spec Cullom, whose horse came clop-a-cloppa up the street right now. Spec jumped out of his green ice wagon and threw a heavy round iron weight on the grass to keep his horse, Nelly, from deciding to go on. She stomped one foot or another and switched her tail to shoo away the flies, but she had to stay.

"What's wrong, Rufus?" he asked. He and Rufus had been friends for a long time. "Waxworks face melting to smithereens? Here!"

Spec went to the back of the wagon and with his big bare hands picked up a jagged piece of ice and offered it to Rufus.

Rufus shook his head. This kindness made the tears flow all the more. He lowered his face on his bare knees so Spec would not see him in this desolate situation.

Spec put the big chunk of ice back in the wagon and picked out two small ones for Rufus and Bennie to lick. Rufus licked his with his face still lowered, and the cool drops trickled down his bare brown legs.

"Well," said Spec Cullom, "what in the name of Sam Hill *is* the matter?"

Rufus looked up. He had gotten hold of himself. He said, "For years me and Joey have looked at a little trolley car in the back of the carbarn. We always wanted to own it. This morning two guys there said me and Uncle Bennie could buy it for one dollar. Joey gave us the dollar he got for helping Mrs. Crowley. Uncle Bennie and me went back to the carbarn with the dollar to buy the little trolley and to get it put in writing. But the guys said they was just jokin'!"

"Just jokin', eh?" said Spec Cullom. "Huh! Some joke! Get

up in my seat. You hold the reins, Rufus. You know how to make her 'gee!' I've finished my rounds. So we'll go down there and take a look around a place where they say, 'Just jokin'."

So, cloppity, cloppity, they trotted to the carbarn.

Outside the carbarn there was a hitching post. Spec Cullom hitched Nelly to this, though she whinnied in dismay at such an unusual change in her daily life. Spec went inside by himself. He told Rufus to stroke Nelly on the nose. He'd be out right away.

"Got to see what's going on in here," he said.

Spec stayed in there quite a while. The boys listened. There was no sound of argument, no loud voices, just some low-voiced conversation going on in the little office where Captain Moody kept track of things.

Then Spec Cullom came out with his brother Jim and Bill, who had made the sale. Bill asked Rufus and Bennie to come into the carbarn, and the entire group walked to the back where the little trolley was.

They were joined right away by Captain Moody, who left a spare workman in his office to keep track of things for a few minutes, and all stood beside the little trolley car.

Captain Moody spoke. "We can't sell this little trolley car. It's an antique. But it can still run. There's going to be a trolley car museum opening up soon down near Lighthouse Point. We promised the people working on this museum that we would donate this trolley to them as a gift from the town of Cranbury. You know all about museums, Rufus. Even *I've* been to The Moffat Museum. And what we have decided to do is to name this trolley car The Rufus M."

Rufus looked up at the man. Maybe he was "just jokin'," too. So he didn't say anything.

The man went on. "At this museum there's going to be a little roundabout trolley track. In the summertime, when the crowds come, sometimes, along with other famous trolleys, your little trolley will make a few rounds on a schedule the museum people will work out. Since it doesn't hold many people, only little children will ride in this little trolley. And I'll put it in my arrangement with those fellows across the harbor that at least once on a Sunday afternoon you and Joey and Uncle Bennie can take it around!"

A slow smile spread over Rufus's face. The man could not be jokin' because it was such a long speech!

"Well," said Captain Moody. "What do you think of all this? In a way, it will be *your* trolley. But that is where it will stay, over there in The Trolley Museum."

"Oh-h!" gasped Rufus. "That's great. Gee! But I don't want it to be named The Rufus M. It should be named The Joey M. That is my big brother, and he discovered the little trolley. He showed it to me. Together, we wanted to own it."

"We can name it The J and R . . . and what about this fellow?" he asked, pointing to Bennie.

"He was with me when we almost bought it," said Rufus. Bill hung his head and so did Jim Cullom. "His name is Uncle Bennie Pye."

"How about this for the name of the trolley then, The J. and R. and U.B. Trolley? Keep people guessing what the dickens that means," said Captain Moody, and everybody laughed.

"On opening day," Captain Moody went on, "the museum people might let you two and Joey run the first trolley around the circle with some museum man along with you. Don't mind him. Might just happen to be an old friend of yours, someone from right here in our carbarn. The first trolley, leading the way, sort of, could be this little Cranbury trolley."

Rufus looked at Jim Cullom. Rufus smiled, and Jim Cullom smiled. "Just might be somebody I know," thought Rufus. "And no one's jokin' now."

"We have a fellow here in Cranbury who paints signs," said Captain Moody. "We'll have him paint a sign for this little trolley. Have it say, "The J. & R. & U.B. Express. They'll list it, *Donated by the town of Cranbury, built . . .*" He paused.

"Circa . . ." said Rufus.

"Yes, *circa 1892*," decided Captain Moody.

"Besides," said the captain of the carbarn, "when the day comes that this little trolley leaves its old track here and heads out for The Trolley Museum, you kids and Joey can go with him. Jim Cullom will go with you and maybe the First Selectman, Mr. John Jones of Cranbury."

"Everybody will laugh and clap their hands to see such a tiny trolley!" said Rufus.

Now everybody was laughing. Just then Joey rode up on his bike. He was stunned when he heard the news. Then he had to laugh, too. He murmured, "The J. & R. & U.B. Express."

The man named Bill, who had said, "Just jokin'," came up to Rufus. "I'm sorry about that dollar business. I didn't think you'd believe me."

"It's O.K.," said Rufus. "Bye!"

As the boys were leaving, Captain Moody came out of his office with two rusty old bent trolley car signs. One said SAVIN ROCK and the other said LIGHTHOUSE POINT. "Choose!" he said.

"You choose," said Rufus to Bennie.

"Lighthouse Point, because I can see it across the harbor from my house," Bennie said.

That made Rufus happy because he and Joey really wanted the SAVIN ROCK sign. The Savin Rock trolleys went past their corner all the time.

"You'd think it was Christmas!" said Rufus. He got on the handlebars of Joey's bike, and Bennie got on the crossbar, and Joey pedaled home to the Pyes' house first, because the clock on the green was beginning now to solemnly ring out twelve o'clock.

"You're on time," said Rufus.

"Oh, wait till they hear this! This trolley-car story, almost as exciting as the day we bought Ginger," said Bennie.

At the Moffats' house Jane was in the kitchen helping Mama make some sandwiches. When she and Mama heard the tale of The J. & R. & U.B. Express landing in a museum, they couldn't go on with their fixing. Everybody had to make his or her own sandwich.

"Jane, we'll get you in on the first ride," Rufus promised. "Mama, too, maybe?" Mama smiled. "See this?" he said. "SAVIN ROCK! A real trolley-car sign! I'm going to tack it on the wall of the museum, Jane, near your handcar man's red-calico handkerchief." This he did. So there was now a new section in The Moffat Museum. They named it ADVENTURE.

Joey and Rufus and Jane sat on the back step and studied the museum. "You know, Joey," said Rufus. "We saved Bikey from the junkman to be in our museum. Now maybe because we always went down to the carbarn and admired the little trolley, we saved it from just rusting away in the far corner of the carbarn."

"Right," said Joey. "Right! Instead of that, it will be an 'artifact' in a museum, The Trolley Museum!"

"Right," said Jane. "An artifact in that museum like Bikey in ours!"

9

STRAW HAT DAY

JOEY AND JANE AND RUFUS WERE RACING AS FAST AS THEY
could to Savin Rock because today was Straw Hat Day. In
Cranbury this great event always took place on Labor Day. On
this day the men of the town threw the straw hats that they
had been wearing all summer into the sea. It was a day of great
celebration.

The Moffats loved Straw Hat Day and always tried to be the first ones to get to the end of Wilcox's Pier in Savin Rock, the best place to view the casting away of the hats.

"Next year you will have a hat to cast away," said Jane to Joey as they raced along.

Joey smiled.

Most straw hats were flat. These were the Panamas. They had wide bands of gros-grain ribbon around the brim, and the bands were of different colors. But most men preferred black or dark blue. Practically all the men of Cranbury put on their straw hats on Memorial Day, May 30, and wore them until Labor Day, the day to cast them into Long Island Sound.

After today you'd see very few men with a straw hat on. Tomorrow out would come the derbies, the homburgs, or the caps with ear flaps tucked inside, ready for the cold and blizzardy weather that was bound to come. Tomorrow it might still be as hot as blue blazes, but it didn't matter. Straw hats had been thrown into the sea. That was the custom.

Mama said she had once talked to a lady from Hungary, who said they had the same custom in that country. There the men cast their hats into the Danube River. So this casting away of straw hats on Labor Day was not just a Cranbury custom. "It is the custom everywhere, perhaps," said Jane, awestricken.

"Would you be put in jail if you wore your straw hat *after* Labor Day?" demanded Rufus. "Is there a law against it?"

"No," said Joey. He laughed. "Just a custom, a Straw Hat Day custom . . . almost as much fun as the Fourth of July."

"No fireworks, though, just straw hats shooting into the air instead of Roman candles," said Rufus. "But fun."

The straw hats, which had been bright and shiny on the Fourth of July, had become sunburned. Some had nicks at the edges as though a bird had pecked at them. At the end of this day, men would have to walk home hatless, even those men who were growing bald and might become sunburned or get freckles on the top of their heads. And of course there were always some men who didn't wear the flat straw hats anyway. They wore larger hats, straw, but shaped like their winter hom-burgs, which were too expensive to just fling into the air. Judge Bell was such a man. But he was always there anyway to watch the more wasteful segment of the population throw away their flat hats.

It was a lovely sunny day. No wonder Jane and Joey and Rufus wanted to be the first ones on the scene and shout, "Hur-rah!" when the first hat went sailing and spinning around and around and then waft down on the water to float and bob up one wave, disappear from sight, and come up on another.

"Who will be the first man to throw in his hat?" Rufus wondered.

Joey just smiled. All along Joey had been holding a flat brown paper bag tightly in his hands. "You must have gotten up at the crack of dawn, even before me and Rufus, and made sandwiches," Jane said admiringly.

Joey just smiled, and they hurried on. The nearer they got to the pier, the faster they walked, and they *were* the first to reach the weather-beaten silvery wooden pier, the longest of all the piers. To the right of it was a large rock, shaped like a whale. Weeds and spindly grass grew between the crevasses. This was Savin Rock, and the entire amusement park was named for it. Many families headed for it with their picnics. The fathers of these families would cast their straw hats in from there; others from beaches all up and down the shore.

Even though they were the first to arrive, the way Joey and Jane and Rufus tore to the end of the pier, you would have thought the entire population was in pursuit, racing for the same spot, the end of the pier. Not so. Looking back, though, they could see people beginning to meander this way and that to their own favorite spots.

The tide was low. Between cracks in the wide flat boards, they could see the mud of low tide and clumps of seaweed.

Now and then a clam spurted a stream of water straight up from under.

"There's one!" exclaimed Rufus, flat on his belly, eyes glued to the crack in the boards. You'd think a clam spurting a fine stream of water up from way down under was as exciting as spotting a shooting star.

They sat down on the end of the pier and dangled their bare tanned legs over the edge. They watched what was going on below them and above them . . . the gulls, the clouds. It was such a clear day, they could see all the way across Long Island Sound. A perfect day for the casting away of straw hats. Only a slight and whimsical breeze was blowing, just enough to make the hats go this way and that when the time came.

Joey decided that he would sit on top of the stumpy rounded wooden pile at the corner of the left side of the pier. Boats from Lighthouse Point across the harbor tied up here. He climbed up, carefully clutching his flat paper bag.

"Do you see a boat coming?" asked Jane.

"Not yet," said Joey.

The little excursion boat went back and forth from Lighthouse Point to Savin Rock. Today some people from Lighthouse Point might want to watch Straw Hat Day here in Savin Rock, while some people here in Cranbury might want to make a big hullabaloo for the family and celebrate over there. But the boat was not in sight.

There was another sturdy pile opposite the one that Joey was sitting on. Usually huge sea gulls sat on top of these piles, which were great lookout spots from where they could watch their fellow gulls with fierce and hostile eyes or fly away, screaming, to snatch a little fish from another gull's beak.

"Shoo!" said Joey to an enormous gull who wanted to sit where Joey was settling himself. He might be King Gull. Then he swooped over to the other pile and made the gull there fly off, and he settled on it. He eyed Joey and the entire world with angry beady eyes.

Joey looked down below him. Seaweed, the kind they liked to pinch and squeeze and make the water in the pods spurt out, was clinging to the piles. When the tide came in, the seaweed would be covered.

"Then it gets to look like mermaid's hair streaming in the water," said Jane.

Joey tried to see if his feet could reach the high-water mark on the pile because if they could, he would then dangle them in the water when the tide came in. But he couldn't. Jane clung to him. "Don't fall in!" she said. Rufus and Jane, since they were sitting on the pier and were closer to the water than Joey, might be able to dangle their toes in it later.

Up on his high pile, Joey held his flat paper bag tightly. Now and then a gull flew over and screamed at the sight of the bag, but Joey shooed him away.

"They smell your sandwiches," said Jane.

Joey laughed.

"What kind did you bring?" asked Rufus.

Joey just laughed again and patted his bag gently.

"Such a funny shape for sandwiches," said Jane. "A pie maybe? A surprise perhaps?"

"Yes!" said Joey. "A grand surprise!"

"I wish that big gull would stay over there where he belongs. Maybe we should eat the sandwiches, and he wouldn't bother us," said Jane. She hid her head under her skirt whenever he swooped too near. She drew her legs under her and sat on them crisscrossed.

"Some gulls do bite," she said, "for no reason at all. The art teacher . . . you know the one we call 'the smiley teacher' . . . told us about an artist friend of hers, a great tall Dutchman. Well, he was just standing on the rocks in Rockport, Massachusetts . . . that far away . . . and a big gull, for no reason at all, suddenly walked up to him and bit his big bare toe that was sticking out of his sandal! Bit the toe of a famous artist from Holland! That's what that gull did!"

King Gull went back to his perch. For a while he stayed there scanning a far distant object that attracted his full attention.

"Maybe," said Rufus, "Rockport gulls bite the toes of artists. Maybe Savin Rock gulls are nicer."

"Think so?" said Jane. "Besides, I'm not an artist." She unwrapped her sun-tanned legs and dangled them over the water, watching her reflection rippling beneath her. They all dangled their legs over the water, and they were very happy. They were hardly aware that people had begun to arrive, a few here, a few there, all the men wearing their straw hats.

The wonderful smell of soft-shell crabs cooking in the stalls along the street behind the piers was wafted to them whether there was a breeze or not. The tempting smell hovered over them and mingled with the salt sea air.

"I'm hungry," said Rufus.

"What *is* in your bag anyway?" Jane demanded. "It's not fair not to tell us . . ."

"Probably a lemon-meringue pie," said Rufus. "That's why he's been holding it so carefully."

Joey only laughed and gently patted it. He put the bag to his face and took a deep breath. "Um-m-m!" he said.

"I wish it had soft-shell crab sandwiches in it," said Rufus. "Let me smell it!"

"Smell!" said Joey. "But smell carefully."

Rufus smelled the bag. Rufus always won in the game of "smells." Blindfold him, hold an onion, a peppercorn, even hard things like mace, and say, "Well, what is it, Rufus?" Rufus always got it right. Now he said as quick as a flash, "It smells like *straw*!"

Joey laughed out loud. "Want to see our lunch?" He carefully took a crisp, brand-new, clean, never-been-worn-before straw hat out of the bag . . . a straw hat for Straw Hat Day.

Rufus and Jane gasped. To switch so suddenly from a lemon-meringue pie to a real straw hat left them breathless. "Are you old enough to wear a straw hat?" asked Jane.

"Sure," said Joey. "I'll be sixteen on the twenty-sixth of September. Anyway, if a fella is old enough to giveth his sister away in holy matrimony . . . and that was way back in June! . . . then he is old enough to giveth his straw hat to the whims and the winds of the sea breezes along with all the other men including Mr. Pennypepper, the judge, and the First Select-man."

The hat had a bright red ribbon around the brim. It could easily be spotted when it was sent skimming over the waves. "Where'd you get it?" asked Jane.

"Crowley's. Saturday, Mrs. Crowley said to me, 'Joey. Choose a hat, any one you want. Be part of your pay. And throw it into the sea. I'll be there and I'll say that there goes Joey in one of my Crowley Department Store hats . . . along with many another!' "

"Put it on!" urged Rufus. "I hear people coming . . ."

"O.K.," said Joey. "It fits fine. It won't blow away. I tried a lot of them on to get one that would stay on."

"Oh, Joey!" exclaimed Jane. "You look great! Too bad you didn't wear your long-pants suit. They'd'a stood you up beside the First Selectman and the judge and the other important people . . .'"

Joey looked around. None of these famous people had arrived yet.

Jane and Rufus looked up at Joey sitting there on top of his pile, and he tipped his hat to them and made a funny face. Then he tipped his hat to the curious gulls, but he hung on to it. No matter how tightly it fitted his head, he didn't want a stronger breeze, a gull, or some mean guy to snatch it away.

Rufus and Jane laughed at his funny faces. "When will you throw your hat in?" asked Jane.

"Be the first?" asked Rufus hopefully.

"Oh, no!" said Joey. "The First Selectman, John Jones, he'll be coming soon, and he'll be first. Next other important people. After that anybody throws."

They looked around. Their pier was beginning to fill up. So

were the others up and down the sound, as well as the beaches
and the big rock, Savin Rock.

"Where do you think your straw hat will land?" asked Jane.

Joey just laughed.

"On Long Island, maybe," said Rufus. "On top of one of
those telegraph poles over there?"

"Or maybe," said Jane, "sail up and up and by tonight land
on the man in the moon. Straw hat from Cranbury, Connecticut, Earth, Universe, lands on the head of the man in the
moon!"

Joey just laughed. "He has a plan," thought Jane.

Out in the water some little boats . . . sailboats, rowboats, a
few cabin launches and motorboats, even some canoes . . . had
moved in, and many had cast anchor out near the breakwater.
From there they would have a wonderful view of the casting
away of the straw hats of the Cranbury men. Perhaps some had
cameras or binoculars!

There was a buoy in the middle of the bay between the
piers and the breakwater and was, as always, clanging its dole-
ful ding-dong, ding-dong as it bobbed this way and that in the
waves.

"Doesn't he look funny, that buoy?" asked Jane.

"Like he's watching the goings-on," said Joey. He took his

hat off now and held it tightly in his two hands.

More and more people began to arrive, crowding onto the pier. Laughing, sauntering, strolling, making up funny stories or limericks about their hats soon to be strewn over the sea, they took up positions in the best possible places.

Even Mr. Buckle came leaning on his cane with one hand and with the other on Miss Nellie Buckle, his daughter, who guided him to the post opposite Joey's. Mr. Buckle did not have a straw hat on. Winter and summer he always wore his Civil War cap.

The band struck up. People shouted, "Hurray!" as the disgruntled gull flew off and settled on the prow of a boat nearby. Then the First Selectman, Mr. John Jones, arrived, and escorted by a man with a megaphone, he made his way through the crowd, bowing to right and to left and tipping his straw hat, the last time it would ever be tipped. When he threw his hat out over the deep blue sea, then it was everybody's chance.

He and the man with the megaphone finally made their way to the place that had been reserved for them, in the middle of the end of the pier. Turning his back to the sea and facing the people, Mr. Jones got ready to say a few words suitable for this special occasion.

But people were still arriving. Judge Bell with his wife and their three little girls came along the pier. Judge Bell had on his usual straw hat, which he had no intention of casting into Long Island Sound.

His three little girls sat down on clean little linen towels Mrs. Bell had brought for this occasion. They squeezed in next to Rufus and Jane. They had on pretty organdy dresses and wore the whitest white stockings Jane had ever seen. She tucked her bare legs under the edge of the pier so the contrast would not be so dramatic.

"I see me in the water!" said Noonie. But that was all that was said, for now the man with the megaphone raised it to his mouth and boomed forth:

"Citizens of Cranbury! Welcome to our annual Straw Hat Day! I have the honor to present the First Selectman of our town, Mr. John Jones, who will say a few words."

Mr. Jones took the megaphone. He tried to say something, but had to wait for the prolonged cheers to end. Many men who had waited long enough and who had been twirling their hats around and around like pitchers warming up for the throw with three men on base shouted, "Hear! Hear!"

Finally, the First Selectman was able to begin. Megaphone in one hand, straw hat in the other, the symbol of this funny, special day, he spoke.

"Welcome, all you hat-throwers with your lovely ladies. Little children, welcome! Be careful not to fall off the pier. There are no railings. Stick close to your mothers. We want hats, not children, to go flying out o'er the great blue sea!"

The First Selectman was quite famous for his limericks, and he had created one for today. Last year's one had been printed in the *Cranbury Chronicle* and, framed, hung in the hallway of the Town Hall. Maybe this one would, too. The new one went like this:

> *Straw Hat Day,*
> *Oh, Straw Hat Day!*
> *Come ye who may*
> *With straw hats, I say,*
> *To cast away*
> *In our Savin Rock Bay!*

Then he wound his hat around and around and finally said, "Farewell, my friend in good weather or foul, this is the end! Ave atque vale!" And with a mighty swing, he flung his hat over the sea!

King Gull snatched it in his beak, and at this astonishing sight, a pause in the great mass of flying hats occurred. At this tense moment, Joey stood up on his post . . . people may have thought this had been a rehearsal . . . wound and wound and wound his hat, and then aiming as straight as an arrow, he flung it high above the sea. Up into the air it went, and it was twirling and spinning around and around as the breeze carried

it toward the buoy that was bobbing as usual between the pier and the breakwater.

"He's aimin' for the buoy!" said Jane excitedly to Rufus, and the word went from mouth to mouth, and men, about to throw their hats in, waited to hear. Had it or hadn't it reached its mark?

It had! It had! Joey Moffat's straw hat had landed on the buoy! So now the buoy, still wailing its mourning, warning sing-song tune, had on a straw hat! It bobbled this way and that and seemed to be tipping its hat to the people in boats as they came nearby to take a snapshot or just to look.

There it stayed. "He looks like a humpty-dumpty buoy with Joey's hat on top." This was passed along from one person to another, and Judge Bell asked to borrow the binoculars that the oldest inhabitant always carried with him to look at some bird. Everybody clapped and said, "Hurray!"

Well, now that that excitement was subsiding somewhat, it was anybody's turn. Whoever wanted to throw his hat in did so.

Straw hats went flying through the air, dozens and dozens of them from all the piers, from the shore and beaches, from the big picnic rock. They spun around. They bumped into each other. They looked like funny birds migrating somewhere. The gentle breeze blew the hats east and west and north and south, for the wind was, as the weatherman had predicted, variable. Then after circling this way and that in the air, one by one the hats fell into the water, where they floated placidly.

"Sea giants could put them on their heads and have an underwater parade down below," said Jane.

The current gathered many of the hats together. "They look like an armada," said Rufus. "Straw Hat Armada invades Savin Rock!" he shouted.

People clapped their hands.

At first the armada headed toward New York, going past Savin Rock. Gulls, enjoying the picnic there, screamed in outrage and took a nip of this hat or that and then perched on one or another of them. They fluttered their wings sometimes to get a better balance, spreading them wide over the flat golden hat boats. This made the gathering of the hats look even more like an armada of small ships with white sails.

Joey asked if he could borrow Mr. Buckle's binoculars. He looked for his hat. There it was all right, with its bright red band, bobbing this way and that on the buoy! The armada had turned itself all around. The tide had turned, and the armada was now on the way out toward the harbor. So people had a chance to cheer and wave at their hats again as they headed

now toward Lighthouse Point and the deeper waters of Long Island Sound.

Joey handed the binoculars back, and they finally reached Mr. Buckle. He observed, "This is an historic armada and, thank heavens, a peaceful one, just giving joy."

The First Selectman took the megaphone and said what a splendid straw hat morning it had been. He would have quickly thought up another limerick, but people were hungry, so he bade them farewell instead.

Some, including the judge and the First Selectman, headed for a fine restaurant; others decided to find a shady spot or to go down to the beach and eat their sandwiches. As the crowd thinned out, again the tempting smell of soft-shell crabs filled the air and spread strongly over the pier, where the Moffats were still sitting.

"H-m-m," said Rufus. "Well, what are *we* going to have for lunch?"

"All along we thought you must have some special sort of flat sandwiches in your bag . . . even apple fritters . . . and it turned out to be a straw hat," said Jane. But she laughed. "The hat was better, much, much better. See it wobbling out there like a man in charge of a grand regatta?"

Joey laughed. "Yes," he said. "Good-by, hat!" Then he looked down at his brother and sister and said, "Want to know what we're going to have for lunch. Take in a big, deep breath with your nose and mouth wide open. Smell!"

"All I smell is soft-shell crabs," said Rufus.

"Me, too," said Jane. "But they cost twenty-five cents each!"

Joey laughed again.

Nonchalantly he took a crisp one-dollar bill out of his back pocket. He waved it at them. "It's soft-shell crabs you want?

Ah! It's soft-shell crab sandwiches you get. Hold my place, Rufus," he said.

What an honor! Rufus climbed up and sat on the high pile, and he and Jane watched Joey walk through the dwindling stragglers. They imagined him lining up in front of one of the soft-shell crab stalls and saying, "Three, please!"

"Criminenty!" said Rufus. He was so ecstatic over the way things were going that he nearly fell into the water. Jane grabbed his two legs, and he managed to straighten himself out.

They waited tensely for Joey's return. "Maybe they have sold out . . . there are so many people!" said Jane.

But no. There Joey came carefully weaving his way so as not to bump into anybody. He had three little paper napkins with, of course, soft-shell crab sandwiches in them! They must still be very hot because he passed them from one hand to the other. Now he was running. He wanted them to be piping hot when he reached Rufus and Jane.

Rufus climbed down and sat beside Jane again. Joey put one of the delicious sandwiches in each of their laps. Then he climbed back up on his high pile again, and they all began to eat!

"Oh!" gasped Jane. "How good!"

"How good!" echoed Rufus.

They ate every crunchy crumb, licked their fingers, wiped

their mouths, and tossed the napkins to the gulls, who screamed with warnings to others and made off with them to settle down on one of the hats of the armada.

"That's to make it interesting," observed Rufus. "So the other jealous gulls will have a good fight over the napkins."

Then they began to talk over the happenings of this great Straw Hat Day.

"Joey, where did you get the dollar, the soft-shell crab dollar?" asked Rufus.

"At Crowley's," said Joey. "Same dollar you couldn't use to buy the little trolley car with."

They all laughed. They dangled their feet over the water and watched their shimmering shadows down below. They lay flat on their stomachs and studied the shallow water beneath . . . little fish, schools of little killies staying away from the gulls. Up above, the sky was a brilliant blue, as brilliant as the water. Far in the distance they could see the boat coming from Lighthouse Point. It must be a sight to see the Cranbury hats sailing out to meet the boat, white wings of gulls spread out like sails.

"M-m-m," said Joey. "But come on. It's time to go home."

People were strolling through the park; some were riding the merry-go-round, and the magic of its music was heard all around.

When the Moffats reached the crowded little street where the food stalls were, Joey said, "Remember, I still have a quarter. We'll buy a soft-shell crab sandwich for Mama. If we hurry . . . run . . . it may still be very hot when we get home!"

Was Mama surprised! They all sat around the kitchen table and watched Mama eat her sandwich. She said, "Oh, my! This is good! It's like long-ago Straw Hat Days with your father . . ."

They told her about Joey's hat, how he had aimed for the buoy . . . "Yes, I remember the buoy," Mama interrupted . . . and how it had landed right smack on the buoy's bell-shaped head.

"Joey, boy," she said. "Joey buoy boy!"

She listened to other happenings . . . the straw hat armada. But they couldn't recall the limerick at the beginning, even though it had been thought up by the First Selectman, Mr. John Jones!

10

COME BACK, JOEY! JOEY, COME BACK!

SCHOOL BEGAN AGAIN THE DAY AFTER STRAW HAT DAY.
Everything started off as usual, clean inkwells, new books,
different teachers to get used to. Now the month of September
was nearly over. Today was Thursday and Monday would be
the first of October and the beginning of "October's bright
blue weather!"

Joey was now in the second year of high school . . . a sophomore! He liked it. He liked the teachers, liked the lessons, studied hard. And besides that, Joey was now sixteen years old. Yesterday had been his birthday, and with one strong whoof, he blew out all the sixteen candles on his chocolate birthday cake! That meant his wish would come true, whatever it was.

Today should have been like any other school day, but it wasn't.

When Jane came home from school, nobody was home. This was strange. Where was Mama? She was almost always there when they came home from school. Sometimes she went to town to shop, but she always told them when she might be late. Jane sat down on the top step of the front porch and waited.

Soon Rufus came running up the narrow walk. He raced past Jane and into the house to get a glass of water. Then he came back and sat down beside Jane. "Where's Mama?" he asked.

There was no need to answer because right then Mama and Joey came up the walk. Joey had on his long-pants suit. Joey's being dressed that way on a weekday was so unusual that Jane knew immediately that an extraordinary thing had happened. It had!

Mama broke the news. She said, "We've been to the Town Hall to ask if Joey, now that he is sixteen, could have permission to leave school and go to work. The First Selectman, Mr. Jones, said that was all right, and he filled out Joey's working papers. Here they are! He shook hands with Joey. He said, 'Good luck, Joey!' Well . . ." Mama gave her shoulders a little hitch, a habit she had lately developed, and went indoors. "I'll put the papers behind the clock in the dining room, Joey," she said as she left.

Jane and Rufus were struck dumb. Joey stood beside them. He seemed to be trying to take all this in, too. He didn't sit down because he had on his long-pants suit, and he just wasn't used to it yet. He didn't say anything. Was he glad or was he not?

Finally Jane asked, awe in her voice and wondering should she ask this question at all or wait to be told, "Do you know where you are going to work?"

"Yes," said Joey. "Yesterday I got the job. In the Yellow Building in New Haven opposite the Union Depot. Where Papa used to work. The man I talked to said he remembered Papa from long ago . . ."

"Wow!" said Rufus. "What're you going to do there?"

"Be an errand boy," said Joey.

"Oh, my!" said Jane.

"How are you going to get there?" asked Rufus. "On the train?"

"Nope," said Joey. "On my bike. But I could go on the train for nothing. I'll have a pass. And after a while I can get passes on the train for the entire family . . ."

"Oh, my!" said Jane again. "We can all go down to see Sylvie for nothing. Now, I know two people on the railroad: first George, the handcar man, and now my brother, my own brother!"

Joey laughed. "I won't be a handcar man. I'll . . ."

". . . run errands," said Rufus. "Carrying important messages . . . maybe to the mayor."

Joey laughed again. He seemed now to be sort of pleased.

Jane said, "You planned all this, you and Mama, and you didn't tell Rufus and me one thing!" She sounded hurt.

"Couldn't," said Joey. "Not until it was all certain."

"It's lucky you have a long-pants suit," said Rufus.

"Yop," said Joey. "But some man, a head man, said to me, 'Joe, you can wear your knickers to work. Easier to get around in than in this good suit.'" And Joey went indoors to change into everyday clothes, leaving Jane and Rufus to ponder this startling piece of news. First, there was Sylvie getting married . . . but they'd sort of suspected that was going to happen. It wasn't sprung on them like this. But now . . . Joey getting working papers!

"We didn't have even one hint," said Jane.

"Not one hint," agreed Rufus. "At least he's not getting married!"

After supper Jane and Joey sat down at the square oak dining-room table to study. Joey opened a book. He seemed to be studying. Jane opened a book, but she was still too stunned to keep her mind on her work and didn't notice that her book was upside down.

Working papers! There they were, a blue ribbon around them, tucked behind the clock on the mantel. "When do you start to work?" Jane ventured to ask.

"Monday," said Joey. "At eight o'clock. But be quiet. I have to study."

Today was Thursday, so tomorrow would be Joey's last day of school!

Now his books were stacked up beside him . . . his second-year high school books, all covered with sturdy brown paper jackets the teacher gave out the first day of school to keep the books clean for next year's class. There was a square printed in ink on the front cover. You put your name, your room number, and the subject of the book in these squares.

At the beginning of school, the jackets were clean and even smelled of the ink that outlined the squares. By the end of the year, they were fuzzy at the edges, had grease spots, maybe blots, or the initials of some boy or girl with a heart drawn around them and an arrow darting through the center.

Joey didn't do that, even though there was a special girl named Mary Foley whose initials he would have liked to write on his book jackets. But he didn't . . . he didn't write them anywhere. He just thought them. You might say they were written on his heart.

Joey tried to keep his mind on his work. He opened his Latin book. Some kids might have just plain quit studying the minute they knew they were not going back to school after tomorrow . . . say, "Whoopie!"

Not Joey! He wanted to get a good mark on his last report card from Union School.

He said to Jane, "Will you ask me the new words in the vocabulary?"

Jane did this. "You got them right," she said.

"I like Latin," said Joey.

"Me, too," said Rufus from the Morris chair where he was sitting, legs flung over the arm. "So did Sylvie. Runs in the family. Amo, amas, amat . . ." He laughed, then turned back to the book he was reading, *The Boy Scouts on Mt. Katahdin*. A good book. He was considering being a Boy Scout boy some day like Sam Doody used to be . . . go up on high places such as Mt. Katahdin or other mountains, like the fellows in this book.

"Veni, vidi, vici," he said, and pressed on with the climbing of Mt. Katahdin. "I came, I saw, I conquered," he murmured.

Joey laughed and went on with his other homework, geometry. "Remember, Jane ... you, too, Rufus ... that when you get to be studying geometry, you say 'pa-*rab*-ola!' Not 'para-*bo*-la,' the way you do."

"Para-*bo*-la sounds better to me," said Rufus. "Like something to ride on down at Savin Rock."

"You'll get used to it," said Joey. "Took me a while. Well, bye! I think I'll go out for a little ride."

"Didn't even ask me to come along," said Rufus. "I wish I could go to work with him. I can run errands faster than anybody, almost as fast as Joey!"

Jane said, "I've been thinkin'. Joey has to go to work. Not many ladies come any more to have Mama make dresses. They make their own now. Hems never hang straight! They look awful coming up the aisle in church. Brides still come, but how many brides are there a year in Cranbury? Not enough to pay for everything ..."

"Right," said Rufus. "Well, I'm going out back ... sit in the sleigh, make a plan. Plans pop into my head sometimes when I sit in the sleigh."

Jane went out onto the front porch. She sat down in the green wicker rocker. Maybe a plan would pop into her head!

She watched the stars beginning to come out here and there. "Ts!" she thought. "If only this were Monday evening! Joey would have gone to work . . . his first day there in a new adventure . . . would have been an errand boy for one complete day and come home." One look at his face as he came riding up would tell whether he had liked it or not. If she asked him that question, and he might say, "Swell!" she would know if it were true or not.

"Oh, let it be true," she prayed. "Let 'Swell!' be true!"

The next morning, Friday, they all left for school as usual. Jane pushed her way through the secret swinging door in the green fence and whistled for Nancy. Off they went, arms around each other.

Jane said, "Nancy! You know what? Today is Joey's last day of school. Yesterday, because he is sixteen, he got his working papers."

"Gosh!" said Nancy.

"He's going to work in the Yellow Building running errands, here or there. He begins his job on Monday."

"Gee!" said Nancy.

Jane could see that Nancy was as impressed as any of the Moffats. She probably thought this was as important as Sylvie's getting married. Nancy squeezed Jane's arm tightly to show she understood that Jane was worried about Joey.

After school Nancy picked up four beautiful red apples that had fallen from one of the trees in her mother's orchard. One for her, one for Jane, one for Rufus and one for Joey. She and Jane sat down on the Moffats' back stoop and waited for the boys; but they didn't come. So they ate their apples, and left the boys' apples on the stoop and went back out through the secret door again to look for some kids to play hide-and-go-seek with, or some game.

Hardly had the gate swung to when Joey did come home. He sat down, piled the paper jackets of his books beside him, picked up one of the apples, took a bite, and began to think about school . . . his last day there. He had an empty feeling, as empty as the book jackets without their books inside them. He reviewed practically every minute of the day in his mind.

Miss Muller! He thought especially about Miss Muller, his home-room teacher. She was his favorite teacher, and he knew, he just knew, that she liked him, even though she never said anything. Joey was a quiet boy. Only a little while ago, when the other pupils had left, she asked him to take the brown paper jackets off his books and store the books in the cupboard. He had done this. So here now were the jackets. He touched them lightly, remembered how she had crossed his name off the lists of pupils who had had copies of those books.

For a while Miss Muller hadn't said much except, "Now,

we'll do this, now that . . ." But when he had finished helping her, she said, "Joey Moffat! I'm going to miss you. I live on George Street. Come and visit me sometime, tell me about what you'll be doing."

Joey nodded and he smiled. "Thank you, Miss Muller. Well, bye!" They shook hands, and he left.

He went into other rooms and turned in his books in each. All the teachers were so nice! History . . . Latin . . . Geometry . . . All the teachers wished him well. All shook hands. They must like him, he thought, in surprise.

Then he came home.

Well now! What a good apple this was! He was nearing the core and spat out a brown seed. A sparrow picked it up. But his mind kept going back to school. That girl, Mary Foley! He had never spoken to Mary Foley. He looked at his shoes when they passed each other in the hall. It dawned on him he might never see her again. In the classroom, what a view he had of her! From where he sat, perfect! His seat was by the window. Her seat was seat one, row one, on the opposite side, by the door. She was errand girl for the teacher. "We're in the same sort of work," thought Joey wryly. Errand girl . . . errand boy.

But a better arrangement could not have been laid out. He could see her from every point of view . . . a side view of her when she was studying, the back of her head when she looked toward the door, her whole pretty face when she stood before the class and recited . . . recited perfectly, never made a mistake. "Make a mistake, have to do it over!" he urged her silently so he could watch her up there in front longer, in her middy blouse and red tie and accordion-pleated plaid skirt! Oh, what a picture she made with the sun streaking across the front of the room and shining on her light hair!

So pretty!

Since he had never spoken to her, not even a "Hello," how then could he say, "Good-by? I'm not coming back!"

Joey threw the core of his apple into the red raspberry bushes. Then, let's see. It was really a funny feeling, a sort of lost feeling, not to have something to do . . . studying, something . . .

Just then Rufus came tearing around the house on his scooter. He had a canvas knapsack on his shoulder.

"Guess what!" he said to Joey. "I got the job. You go to work? I go to work. That's fair."

"Yeh?" said Joey. "What job?"

"Delivering the *Saturday Evening Post*. Hughie Pudge got me the job. You know Hughie Pudge? He can't do it any more . . . used to be his job. But now he has to take piano. He says the guy at the *Cranbury Chronicle*, well, this man . . ."

"Name of Mr. Gilligan. I remember *him* all right!" said Joey.

"Yes, same one. Well, he's in charge of seeing that the *Saturday Evening Post* gets delivered as well as his own *Cranbury Chronicle*. He'll have a stack ready for me to put in this sack of mine. And *my* beat . . . they call the route a *beat* . . . is handy. From Elm Street to Main Street and from Savin Avenue to First!"

"Wow!" said Joey, impressed. He handed Rufus his apple.

Rufus ignored it; he had more to tell. "Want to know how it happened? I just happened to bump into Hughie. He asked me if I wanted the job.

"First I asked Hughie, 'You need working papers for this job from the people at the Town Hall?'

" 'Sure you need working papers,' he said. 'But not from the Town Hall. I have your working papers. It's a contrack. Rain or shine, I have to deliver the *Saturday Evening Post*. Give this contrack,' Hughie said, 'to Mr. Gilligan. Tell him I'm willing you my route because I have to take piano. I already told him about you. Says he knows you . . . knows Rufus Moffat.'

"So," said Rufus, "I went over to the *Cranbury Chronicle*, and Mr. Gilligan said, 'How old are you, Rufus?'

"Same age as Hughie," I said. "And I handed him Hughie's contrack willing me the route. I told him Hughie and me were

in Grade One together in Wood School and have stayed together all the way through school. We are now in Grade Four.

" 'O.K., Rufus,' he said. 'The job is yours. Here's your canvas sack with *Saturday Evening Post* engraved on it!' And he
gave me a list of the people that get the magazine. You know
who's on my list? Just some of them? Judge Bell, the Pyes, the
Stokes . . . gosh! The list is a little messed up. Jelly on it. I
didn't put it there. Hughie must have."

Rufus took a bite of his apple. "Where's Jane?" he asked.

At this moment, as though by magic, Jane pushed her way
through the swinging door in the fence. She said, "Behold!" for
no reason that her brothers could see. They didn't know that
she had just been playing the game of Ladies Fainting and
now, when she heard the news of Rufus's contract and job, she
went into a pretend swoon and said, "The smelling salts,
please."

Recovering, she said, "My, Rufus! That's great!"

Then Rufus climbed up on the sleigh and sat there proudly,
empty canvas sack beside him, reins in hand. "In the olden
times maybe they delivered the *Saturday Evening Post* by
sleigh in the winter," he said, and ate his apple up there. "If I
had a pony, I'd give him the apple," he said.

Jane laughed. "Waxworks boy eats apple in sleigh. Could be

a picture in a book." Then she said, "I came home early because I got to thinking about the museum."

"Yeah," said Rufus. "Who's goin' to be the guard, count the people, keep an eye on the star dust, the flies, the Savin Rock trolley sign . . . any artifact . . . when Joey goes off to work?"

"That's why I came home," said Jane. "In the middle of the game of Fainting Ladies, Nancy Stokes was in the middle of a swoon at that moment, the same thought struck me, so I rushed home before she got the salts, even."

"A coincidents . . ." said Rufus.

"Yeah," said Jane. "We have to get the sleigh back inside the museum, put everything to the side . . . the easel, the costumes . . . The heads can stay on the wall and some other artifacts. Let's get the doors from the side of the barn and stand them up. I think the hinges are too rusty to try to make them fit. Let's make a sign that will say . . . well, just say . . ."

Rufus said, "Jane, you thought the museum up. Now you're thinking it down. It makes sense."

"I am *not* thinking it down," said Jane indignantly. "The museum is special, and we'll always have it. We'll just make a sign, a polite sort of a sign, like this, maybe: THE MOFFAT MUSEUM CLOSED FOR THE COLLECTING OF MORE ARTIFACTS!"

It didn't take long to follow through with this plan. And it was much easier to slide the ancient sleigh back inside than it had been to drag it out. No ropes around Rufus's waist were needed. Rufus stuffed crumbly old tissue-paper patterns Mama gave them into the sleeves of his little old mackinaw and also in the old gray woolen cap. "Them's my brains," he said. Then he put his quite twisted wax face in between the cap and the scarf. "Just having sad thoughts," he commented, "going over a frozen riverbank or seeing a hungry dog loping along. Who knows?"

But they removed the humped-up-in-the-middle rag rug Catherine-the-cat had enjoyed all summer and brought it back indoors and put it on the Morris chair in the dining room where it always used to be. Instead, they put in the sleigh some old warm rags Mama was going to sell to the ragman on his next tinkling trip down Ashbellows Place, and these did nicely. So, now there he was, Rufus, the waxworks boy, an imitation of him anyway, as he had been when he made his debut during the famous visitation of the children on tour with Mr. Pennypepper.

The silvery gray wooden doors leaning now against the front of the museum had a few knotholes in them. People could peek in. Rufus did so. He laughed. "I see me!" he said. "Rufus, the waxworks boy! My, how he has shrunk! We'll say, 'Waxworks statues have a habit of shrinking in cold weather. Come summertime, they puff out again!' "

"They'll think, 'My, how much you know!' " said Jane.

"And all because I clapped the erasers that day in the schoolroom and rubbed off the name Madame Tussaud from the blackboard! I'll stand beside the peephole when people peek in. I'll say, 'Peek in, you non-believers! Here *I* am, the real Rufus. And *there* I am, a Madame Tussaud waxworks me.' I hope Letitia Murdock will come and stare . . ."

"M-m-m," said Jane. "But not often, I hope."

Joey made the sign and tacked it up. There it was! CLOSED FOR THE COLLECTING OF MORE ARTIFACTS!

Then Joey sat down on the back step again, took a crumpled newspaper clipping out of his pocket, and studied it carefully.

"What's that?" asked Jane.

"An ad from some school out west that I'm going to study with nights. You send the lessons in by mail."

"O-o-oh!" said Jane in excitement.

"What will you study?" asked Rufus. "Latin?"

"Nope," said Joey. "How to be a draftsman."

"What's that?" asked Jane.

"Drawing plans. Plans for houses, factories, telephone equipment. Gosh, I don't know what all yet . . ."

In bed that night Jane began to feel better about Joey's leaving school because he'd still be learning . . . by letters, by mail. But when she woke up on Monday morning, her heart was heavy again. Did Joey really like the idea of going to work or was he pretending?

She hopped out of bed, dressed, and went downstairs. Everyone was up early. Joey had to leave by seven-thirty so he would be on time.

"And," said Rufus, "you have to allow lots of time in case the Cumberland Avenue Bridge is up for some boat or a string of barges to go through."

"O-o-oh!" said Jane. "Like me on the eight-fifteen waiting for the drawbridge over the Housatonic to come down. Oh, I hope that doesn't happen to you, Joey, on your first day of work!"

Everybody ate breakfast in a hurry. Then Joey folded back the bottoms of his long pants with clamps so they would not get caught in the spokes of the wheels and got on his bike.

Mama handed him his lunch. He put the brown paper bag in the leather tool chest attached to the back mudguard, and he was ready. Mama kissed him good-by. He rang his bell three times and started off.

Jane ran after him. "I'll wave from the corner," she shouted.

Joey didn't look back, but he had heard. He held up one hand, waved, and sped down Elm Street. At the corner of New Dollar Street he turned his head, saw Jane standing at the curb of Ashbellows Place, and waved once more. Then on he went, growing smaller and smaller. Jane stood up and danced up and down and waved and waved, but he was just a small speck in the distance now. Then she couldn't see him any more.

Jane began to cry. "Come back, Joey! Joey, come back!" she sobbed. "Joey! Joey!"

Jane mopped her eyes on her petticoat, went home, got her books, kissed Mama good-by, went through the secret door, whistled for Nancy, and off to school they went, arms around each other's shoulders. Jane couldn't help it. Tears kept rolling down her cheeks, and she didn't have a handkerchief.

Nancy pretended not to notice, but she tucked her handkerchief in the pocket of Jane's sweater.

In school, Miss Mason, the teacher, did what she always did the first thing in the morning. She read a chapter of a good book. They had just finished *Tom Sawyer*. Now she was reading *Heidi*.

Wasn't it lucky this was such a sad story? No one would think it was odd that tears kept falling down Jane's cheeks. Some other children might be crying, too, from the sad story, not from such a sight as watching a brother disappear from sight, going toward the Cumberland Avenue Bridge, going to work, starting a different sort of life.

On the way home from school, Nancy, knowing that Jane was sad, said, "Let's go to town and watch old Mr. Natby shoe horses. See the sparks of the anvil fly?"

Jane pondered. The trolley car would go past the Yellow Building where she might catch a glimpse of Joey running lickety-split on an important errand. Even so, she said, "No. I don't think so, Nancy. I can't go. I have to wait at the corner for Joey."

"O.K.," said Nancy. "See you later."

Jane went home, kissed Mama hello, put her books on the dining-room table, and tore down the street to the corner. She sat down on the curb at Elm Street, ate an apple, and prepared herself for the long wait for Joey. She would watch him beginning as a speck and then coming nearer and nearer. She didn't care how long it took. She wanted to think about Joey anyway, and she wanted to be right here at this corner when Joey came riding home. She wanted to look at his face. Had he liked the way the day had gone or hadn't he? She had to know.

If Rufus had not all of a sudden gotten so many jobs . . . delivering not only the *Saturday Evening Post*, but also the *Cranbury Chronicle* . . . he would be sitting here beside her, watching the trolley cars, waiting for Joey.

Jane pondered. "I must think of some way to earn money, too. Earn it, tuck it in Mama's black pocketbook that she hangs on the knob of the kitchen door, say, "Mama! Look inside! Lots of money . . . enough to buy a clarinet for Joey, maybe?" And perhaps something for everybody else. How? Well, that idea would have to pop itself into her head, all unexpectedly, the way ideas tended to do.

"Look at this!" Mama would exclaim. And Jane would laugh and hug her.

Well, it was getting late now. People coming from town were getting off the trolley cars. Some got off at Ashbellows Place. Jane knew most of them, but most did not notice Jane sitting on the curb. She wondered if any of them had noticed a big boy, her brother, Joey Moffat, riding home on his blue bike? But she didn't ask. You don't ask a tired man a question, even friends like Mr. Price.

O-o-h! He would be coming soon. She stood up and peered closely far, far down the street. There! Sure enough! There he was! She was sure that that little speck in the distance was Joey, coming closer and closer. It was . . . it certainly was . . . Joey!

Jane waved and waved. She danced up and down. She waved the red tie from her middy blouse. Joey saw her. From way way down at New Dollar Street he saw her! He waved. Closer and closer he came. He was speeding. He waved again, and he rang his bike bell. He rode with both hands, with one hand and with no hands, swinging his arms in the air! Then, with both hands on the handlebars, he crossed the trolley tracks and put on the brakes right in front of Jane, making the dirt fly the way he did at home in their backyard. This time Jane didn't care.

Jane laughed and Joey laughed. His face was shining. One look was enough for Jane. He had liked what he had done at work, liked having his working papers, liked being an errand boy for the New York, New Haven, & Hartford Railroad Company!

Jane hopped up, and they rode slowly home. "Was it fun being an errand boy?" she asked. "Carrying important messages? Like maybe telling somebody that the eight-fifteen might be late? Or a message to some banker on the Bankers' Express?" At least, so she thought. But who could tell what a quiet boy like Joey really thought deep down inside himself?

"I don't know. I don't see the messages. Mostly it's carrying supplies here or there. But I've only been there one day," he said.

They rode home. Mama was waiting for them on the front porch. She kissed Joey, took a long look at his face, smiled, and said, "You must be hungry . . . all that long ride!"

"Three miles!" said Joey.

Just then Rufus came racing up the narrow path, his empty wagon bumping along crazily behind him because one of its wheels was wobbling, almost rolling off. "Joey," he said, "you beat me home!"

He pulled his wagon around back and then joined them again. "That wheel! It kept coming off. It came off in front of Judge Bell's house. He was sitting on his front porch reading the *Cranbury Chronicle*. He took a piece of string out of his pocket and tied it on for me. I'm always, even when I am grown, going to carry a piece of string in my pocket, just like Judge Bell. After supper I'll fix it right. Did you like your job, Joey?"

"Yop," said Joey.

"Me, too," said Rufus.

What a day for everybody! They went indoors, and a big

surprise awaited Joey. Mama handed him a long cardboard roll filled with . . . Jane and Rufus waited and wondered, but Joey knew. "It's marked, 'Lesson One: SCHOOL OF DRAFTSMAN-SHIP! Open carefully,' " Mama said.

"Wowie! It came," exclaimed Joey. "I sent for it and it came! Nobody touch this!"

Rufus and Jane backed to the wall.

"I'll open it after dinner," said Joey.

And what a dinner! Pork chops, apple sauce, succotash, and mashed potatoes with gravy, and some enormous round cookies with scalloped edges for dessert!

After dinner, Jane and Joey sat down at the dining-room table. There wasn't one crumb on it. Rufus sat in the Morris chair, legs flung over the arm.

Then Joey carefully pulled the slender string that made the cardboard roll unwind, and there was Lesson One! After studying the instructions, he spread out a sheet of pale translucent blue drawing paper. It was large.

Joey said, "They send you two sheets of this special paper because if you make one tiny mistake, you can't send it in. They don't want any erasings, even though they sent a special eraser . . . for a crisis, I suppose."

A kit had come in a separate small box. It had, besides the

eraser, a bottle of India ink, a special pen, a sextant, and a steel ruler. He lined these up on his right.

"A college boy!" thought Jane proudly.

Joey rolled up his shirt sleeves and prepared to begin Lesson One.

"Here beginneth the first lesson," said Jane solemnly, like

the Reverend Mr. Gandy in the pulpit. She prepared to do her own homework and opened her arithmetic book.

But Joey said, "Jane, you'll have to do your homework somewhere else. You might joggle the table. Lucky I haven't dipped the pen in the India ink and made a blot right to begin with! I told you, it has to be absolutely perfect."

"Oh!" said Jane. "I'm sorry." She felt like crying. How could she have been so stupid? Of course a person can't draw fine lines with someone joggling the table.

Rufus unwound himself from the Morris chair. "You can have my seat," he told Jane. "I have to fix my wagon, and he tiptoed out of the room, remembering to avoid the loose board behind the table.

So Jane sat down in the Morris chair. Its wide arms made of pretty cherry wood were perfect for writing on and doing homework. She glanced at Joey. He was absorbed in his work. He looked happy.

Jane soon finished her homework and tiptoed out the room, avoiding, as Rufus had, stepping on the loose board, not breathing until she got outside and joined Rufus.

Rufus was glad to have some help. He said, "Hold the wagon steady while I screw on this baby carriage wheel I found in a lot. Luckily it matches the one on the other side. Jane, you keep your eyes out for spare wheels. This job I have is going to put my wagon under a big strain! It will have to be an artifact for the museum soon."

Then Joey came to the back door. "Hey!" he said. "Wanna see what I did before I wrap it up?"

Jane and Rufus tore into the house. But when they reached the dining room, they tiptoed as though a fragile work of art was in there and might fall or be injured.

Joey held up his blue sheet . . . Lesson One. There was a square on the lower right-hand corner. Joey had drawn this square and in it had printed his name, his address, and Lesson One. It was ready to go.

"My! That's pretty," said Jane. "And you didn't make a mistake because there's the spare one still there. But if you ever do make a mistake and do have to use the spare sheet, can we have the no-good one for the museum, tack it on the wall near the easel? It's pretty enough to frame."

"They'll get prettier and harder the more lessons you get into," said Joey. "I hope they come along fast. I love doing this!"

Jane and Rufus watched, from a distance, as Joey rolled the drawing up and inserted it inside a cardboard tube that had also come with the supplies. It fitted neatly in this, and Joey put a two-cent stamp on it. Then, with Rufus on the crossbar holding the document carefully, he rode off on his bike to the post office. Joey figured that if he got it in the mail tonight, it would go off on the early train first thing in the morning.

"Maybe on the eight-fifteen! That has a mail coach on it!" said Jane. And she watched them ride off.

Now what was Jane going to do? That's what she wondered. She went inside. Mama was sitting in the living room reading the *Cranbury Chronicle*. Jane went back to the dining room and sat down at the table. What should she do? Oh, she knew! She would write a letter to Sylvie. She would try to make it funny so Sylvie would not be homesick. She opened up her Elm City pad with its blue-lined paper and began her letter.

Dear Sylvie:

How are you? And Ray, how is he? Do you still like it where you live? I like it, and I'll visit you again some day if you want me to. We are all fine. Guess what? Joey went to work today. He got his working papers last Thursday. He goes to work on his bike. Today was his first day. He said he liked it. He is an errand boy in the Yellow Building. Remember where that is . . . on Meadow Street in New Haven across the street from the depot? I said, "How do you like it there, Joey?" He said, "Fine." I am going to wait for him at the corner every day for him to come back. I did that today.

I miss you. Oh, the bed seems empty without you. I spread

my arms and legs all across it and try to fill it up. Oh, it's going to be cold in the wintertime without you in it. Sometimes, I can't get to sleep right away. I think, "My! How late Sylvie is tonight at choir rehearsal!" Then I remember you are not coming home.

Guess what! Rufus inherited Hughie Pudge's Saturday Evening Post route. He has a big canvas bag and he delivers them and he also delivers the Cranbury Chronicle. And he is also going to sing in an all-boys choir in a big church on the New Haven green. He gets paid for it. Can you imagine getting paid for singing? Mama says it is the custom. The minister there told Rufus he knows Ray and said to say, "Hello." So, "Hello!"

We got our report cards today for the month of September. You remember they rank you in Room Thirteen? Mae Stevens ranked first. I didn't know she was so smart. I ranked third. Nancy Stokes ranked fifth. Wouldn't it be funny if a dummy like me ever got to rank first sometime? Ha-ha!

Miss Mason, my teacher now, remember? Well, she said to say "Hello" to you. So, "Hello." I picked up Joey's report card from Miss Muller. Remember her? The card said on the bottom of it Final Report, and the teacher had drawn a line across the rest of the report card from upper left to lower right sidewise all the way from October through June. No Joey in school all those months. She wrote on the bottom of it . . . you re-

member the way she writes? So even? She wrote, "Good luck, Joseph Moffat. We will miss you. Your teacher, Miss Anna V. Muller." Joey smiled when he saw it. He put it in his pocket, the one in the inside of his new coat, the coat of the suit he wore to your wedding. Remember? I think he's going to keep it there always unless his pocket gets filled up with the names of places he has to run back and forth to, being an errand boy. Mama didn't have to sign his report card on the back because he isn't going back. But she signed it anyway . . . Mrs. Catherine G. Moffat. She said the report card looked funny without her name on it. Joey thought so, too.

Were you wondering about the museum now that Joey has gone to work? Well, we moved the sleigh back inside the barn. Your easel with the drawing of the fox with the bushy tail is in a new place close to the wall. It looks pretty there. Rufus put his waxworks head . . . it's grown a little lopsided . . . and all the clothes that Rufus, the waxworks boy, wore in the sleigh, a wintertime scene, a Madame Tussaud statue . . . you notice I know how, we all know how, to spell that? Well so, yes. He put himself, his waxworks self, in the sleigh, so if people look through the knot in the wood of the door . . . we found the doors and stood them up . . . well, the knots make peepholes. People can see there really was a Madame Tussaud waxworks boy, especially if Rufus happens to be standing alongside that person peeping in. Real Rufus outside, waxworks statue inside. From now on our museum is going to be just for us Moffats, our special museum, not one for the entire population. That is the way I meant it to be in the beginning. Remember? It all just started with your old brown bike.

It's late. I hear the boys coming home. I hear Joey's bike bell. He just mailed Lesson One to a school far away. He is learning to be a draftsman. Then he will not run errands all his life. He will draw wonderful plans. Oh, I waved him good-by this morning. I'll always wave him good-by. And I'll always wait for him at the corner and wave him "Hello" when he comes riding back. I hope he always says, "Fine," when I ask him how it was there today in the Yellow Building.

> *Your loving sister,*
> *Jane*

Jane showed Mama the letter. "It's not very funny," she apologized. "I know Sylvie likes funny letters so she can say Ha-ha a lot. Perhaps I should put a few more Ha-ha's in it?"

Mama read the letter. "You don't always have to write a funny letter. This is a good letter . . . full of news, the kind of news that Sylvie will love to hear," Mama said.

Then Mama put the small kerosene lamp in the window in the hall. What a busy day! What a day! Everyone was tired out.

Mama kissed them all good night. The boys went upstairs to bed. Jane stood at the foot of the stairs for a moment. She saw Mama go back into the parlor and put the iron rod in the very last notch of the green-velvet Morris chair. Then, half reclining, she looked out the window, the way perhaps she often did, looking at the room outside, an exact reflection of the room inside. Maybe sometimes she imagined someone coming into that room outside, maybe, half asleep, she might imagine . . . maybe . . . Papa?

"Good night, Mama," Jane whispered and tiptoed up the stairs to bed.